Paper & Kindling

A 3-4-1 Collection

Stories / Poems by:

Christine Ricketts
Nicole DeGennaro
Kaitlyn Sudol
Lara Eckener

With art by:

Katie Grosskopf
Alex Griggs
Cleopatria Peterson

Paper & Kindling: A 3-4-1 Collection

This book contains works of fiction. All names, characters, places, and events are either products of the authors' imaginations, or are used fictitiously. Any resemblance to actual events, locales, or persons—living or dead—is entirely coincidental.

Copyright Acknowledgements

© 2016 by Christine Ricketts / Art by Christine Ricketts
      A Room for Death
      Out of Uniform
      A Quiet Anger
      Dear Author

© 2016 by Nicole DeGennaro / Art by Katie Grosskopf
      Return to Form
      Mortal Coil
      Alternate Ending
      The Modern Phoenix

© 2016 by Kaitlyn Sudol / Art by Alex Griggs
      First Date
      Vacation (all I ever wanted)
      Countdown
      Coat Check

© 2016 by Lara Eckener / Art by Cleopatria Peterson
      Temple Break
      Memory
      Shadow
      Refurbished

Paper & Kindling: A 3-4-1 Collection
Copyright © 2016 by 3-4-1 Publications
ISBN 978-0692813249

Cover design by Alex Griggs

To never losing hope, even when hope feels lost.
- Christine

To those who need fortitude, may you find it in these pages.
- Nicole

Table of Contents

About the Authors

Christine Ricketts has been writing for as long as she can remember and boy, are her hands tired. She also enjoys reading, playing video games and theoretical attempts at organization. On rare occasions she will do something involving that so-called "reality" people are always talking about. She doesn't really see the appeal.

Nicole DeGennaro is a human being who exists. Sometimes. When she isn't toiling over the written word, she is often wasting time on the Internet or annoying her cats. She also takes on way too many projects for her own good, but she enjoys all of them. You can learn more about all that at her virtual Batcave: http://nicoledegennaro.wordpress.com/.

Kaitlyn Sudol is an aspiring children's author with a boring day job. She lives in the Boston area where she spends a lot of time having brunch and talking about horror movies, comic books, musical theatre, and kidlit. When she's not reading, writing, or brunching, she's probably recording an episode of The Worst Bestsellers or mindlessly refreshing the internet. You can hear her complain about the MBTA at @fourteenacross on Twitter or hear her talk about literature of questionable quality at www.worstbestsellers.com.

Lara Eckener loves poetry, comics, and poetry about comics. You can find her work in *Drawn to Marvel: Poems from the Comic Books* and *Strange Romance Volume 2.* She talks about all manner of media and feelings on twitter as @LaraEckener.

About the Artists

Katie Grosskopf is a Brooklyn-based illustrator and blogger whose interests include petting every dog in sight, figuring out public transportation in foreign places, learning about dinosaurs, strategically packing suitcases, and eating pizza. Her work and latest adventures can be found at www.seekatiedraw.com.

Katie provided the art for "Mortal Coil", "Return to Form", "Alternate Ending" and "The Modern Phoenix."

Alex Griggs is a print and pattern designer from Indiana, who now works and lives in New York City. When she isn't playing soccer or trying to keep up with her marathon-running mother, she is happiest at home playing video games alongside her cats.

Alex provided the art for "Vacation (all I ever wanted)", "Coat Check", "First Date" and "Countdown."

Cleopatria Peterson is an illustrator and comic artist based in Toronto, Canada. She graduated Ryerson University with a bachelor's of design and has been published in the Toronto Comic Anthology. She loves lending her art to all forms of storytelling.
www.cleopatria.ca
http://cleopatriia.tumblr.com/

Cleopatria provided the art for "Memory", "Refurbished", "Shadow" and "Temple Break."

Acknowledgements

Christine would like to thank Nicole, Kaitlyn and Lara for believing her when she said this would totally be a good idea. She would also like to thank the future time travelers that she hopes are coming to correct 2016.

Nicole would like to thank Sangsook Pak for once again being an astute and careful proofreader and first reader, and she would like to thank all the other writers and the artists of Paper and Kindling: you have all contributed something wonderful and meaningful to this anthology; I am better for knowing you, and your work has inspired me.

Kaitlyn would like to thank Naomi for reading and editing all of her stories in this collection and Becca for not killing her in her sleep (yet).

Lara Eckener would like to thank Melissa Dominic for her wise words and poetry smarts and Alli Martin for being a constant source of sanity and writerly support.

Introduction

In 2015 I convinced two of my friends to help me put together a collection of short stories that we would then self-publish. I'm the type of person that tends to start projects and never actually finish them so for me, having two cohorts was a great way to ensure I managed to drag myself over the finish line so to speak. Also collaboration is great and friendship is magical and blah, blah, blah.

Mostly it was the finish line.

The idea of the collection was that we would each write one story and then, after reading each other's stories, would write two more stories using those first stories as inspiration. There would be nine stories all together. Three main stories, plus two, plus two, plus two, yep equals nine.

Whew, grade school math for the win!

I took that idea one step further and thought it might be interesting if we had some artists illustrate each of the stories with a similar theme in mind. We teamed each artist up with one of the authors and, after completing the work for the first story, had them check out the other artists' work and take inspiration from those pieces to incorporate into the other two illustrations they did.

That makes sense right?

Anyway, after a bunch of writing, a lot of nagging emails, fighting with layouts and epub creation, a couple of batches of proofs and some very late nights, we managed to pull together our collection, entitled "3-4-1: Three Tales Told Nine Ways".

And luckily, Chris and Nicole still wanted to be friends with me afterwards.

Since it was so much fun the first time I figured, might as well go ahead and do it again! Only this time I decided that instead of three authors, we'd have four. And instead of just stories, we'd include some poetry as well. That meant four artists as well. And instead of one portal to another dimension, we'd open—

Wait . . . forget about that last part.

That means in this collection you'll find twelve stories, four poems and sixteen pieces of art, all of which drew some measure, small or large, of inspiration from each other.

Enjoy!

Part I

Death

1. The end of the life of a person or organism.
2. The personification of the power that destroys life.

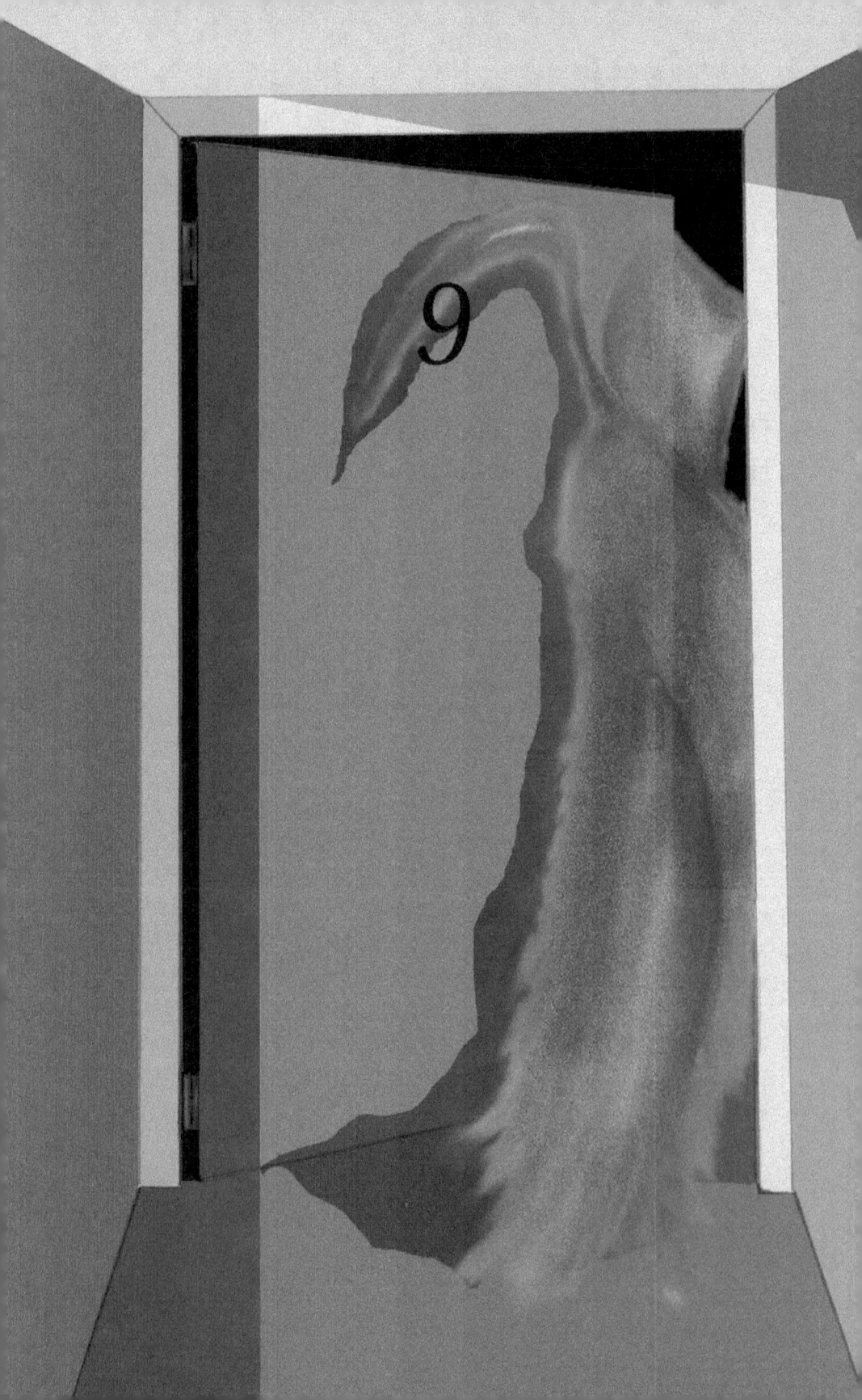

A Room for Death

Christine Ricketts

S ome rooms are never meant to be gone into.

My family owned a hotel—just a small one. Only eight rooms. Technically there were nine but that last room was never booked. Or maybe it's more accurate to say that it was always booked, just seldom occupied.

I don't know when I first started paying attention to it. It seemed like suddenly one day I was changing the sheets in room nine when I realized that I had never seen anyone actually occupy it. I asked my father about it—he said that I was wrong. That every room was always used and that I just never happened to see the customer. Not surprising, considering how often I skived off doing my chores.

But when I asked my mother, she had a different answer—room nine was reserved for a very special someone and we had to make sure it was always available in case that customer showed up. When I asked who it was, thinking someone rich or famous, she only pressed her lips to my forehead and told me that I would know if I ever saw him. Then she added, so quietly that I nearly didn't hear her, *I hope you don't see him for a long time.*

At first, I ignored it—what did I care who took the room? If it was someone famous, it probably wasn't anyone that I knew about. More likely it was one of those old people that my parents thought were cool.

Still, I found myself skipping out on chores less and less, spending more of my free time helping with check-ins, a process that I had previously avoided whenever possible. I took phone calls—even worse—and reservations and greeted strangers pulling in for the night. Every time my dad sent me back into the small office for a room key I waited for him to tell me to grab number nine off its peg.

He never did.

One night all eight rooms were booked, a rare occurrence, and a young couple pulled in out of a storm. I had been watching lightning flash through the front windows when the doors swept open and a man and a woman were all but blown inside. They struggled up to the desk while I muscled the door shut behind them.

"—very sorry. But I'm afraid we don't have any rooms available," I heard my father saying.

"Nothing at all?" the woman asked, sounding very tired.

"We'll take anything," the man added, equally as exhausted.

My father shook his head. "No, we're completely—"

"What about room nine?" I asked, heading towards the storage closet in the lobby where the cleaning supplies were kept. The couple had brought a good portion of the storm inside with them, and the white tiles were in desperate need of a mop.

I knew room nine was open; the key had been hanging alone on the office board when I had grabbed the key for six only a half hour earlier.

I slopped the mop onto the floor and looked up. There were twin looks of relief spreading across the couple's faces. The expression on my father's face was quite the opposite.

"No!" he snapped sharply. He caught himself and offered the couple a tight smile. "I'm afraid that one is also occupied."

But that couldn't be. No one but that couple had called or been in during the last half hour.

"But—" I started. My dad's eyes shot to me. I had never seen him look so angry before.

"We'll pay extra," the woman offered. She flinched slightly when my father's gaze returned to her, still burning.

"As I said—"

"Well, the guest in nine is all settled in now," came my mother's voice. She stepped into the room as if completely unaware of the current discussion. She stopped at the sight of the young couple and made a sympathetic noise.

"Oh, I'm afraid you've caught us with a full house. And with such a storm going on. We hate to have to send you back out into it but there is a motel just a few more miles north. They have more rooms, so they're

4

more likely to have something available. In fact, why don't you give them a call, honey, and see if they have a room?"

My father's smile was tight again but he made the call and sure enough there was plenty of space at the old motel. She had my father take the couple back out to their car under his big umbrella, supposedly to give them directions and make sure they got off okay. But the minute the door shut behind them, she took hold of my arm and knelt down in front of me.

"But no one has checked into nine," I protested before she could speak. I knew that—I'd been on the desk all day, even during my lunch break. My mother inhaled deeply and let her breath out slowly with a smile I was just beginning to recognize as tired.

"Sweetie, it's hard to understand now but it'll make more sense when you're older. I know you hate it when I say that," she added, even as I was opening my mouth. "But for now it's just very important that room nine is always available."

"So it isn't booked right now, is it?" I pointed out hotly. I heard the sharpness in my tone and expected a scolding in turn. But even as I was starting to drop my eyes guiltily to the floor, my mother was turning to look out the window at the storm.

"As a matter of fact, I did just check in a guest," she replied quietly.

I frowned. "But I didn't see anyone come to the desk."

Another tired smile. "He doesn't always check in at the desk."

"How am I supposed to know who to check into room nine if I never see him?" I protested. My mother stood up and, ruffling my hair lightly, turned me so that I was facing the hallway off the lobby.

"Don't worry, you'll know. Now go to bed. There'll be lots to do in the morning."

I thought about protesting; it wasn't even technically my bedtime, but she had already moved behind the desk, her fingers shuffling through papers.

Dragging my feet, I shuffled into the hall. It branched in three directions: to the right were our living quarters, straight ahead were rooms one through four, and to the left were rooms five through nine, with nine at the very end. I glanced down to the left just before I turned to go to my room.

I stopped and looked back.

The hallway was empty. But for a moment, just out of the corner of my eye, I thought I had seen someone outside room nine.

With the storm raging outside and lightning flashing ominously through the windows, there was nothing that could have convinced me to go down the hallway that night. I waited until morning, with the sun streaming in, before I ventured out to look. The door was already open and my mother was inside, standing in the center of the room. I thought for a moment that she was speaking with someone; there was the faint suggestion of a voice that wasn't hers.

The television was on, and my mother was watching the screen intently.

"—two dead in a tragic accident just off route 87—"

Her eyes lifted and she saw me standing in the doorway. The television clicked off. She set the remote down on the end table.

"Um . . . do you . . . need help?" I asked nervously because while she didn't look mad, she didn't exactly look thrilled to see me there.

She shook her head. "No, I'm all finished," she said, even though she didn't have the cart with the turnover supplies.

Room nine was a constant mystery to me; one I spent an untold number of hours trying to solve without alerting Mom or Dad to my intentions. It was pretty clear that whatever the deal was, neither of them wanted me to know. But I was determined.

The answer came sooner than I expected and from a direction I hadn't considered. If it would have changed the outcome, then I would have given anything not to have known.

When I was twelve, my mom got sick. Just a small lump they said at first. They could remove it and treat her and everything would be fine. Each time that she went back the treatment got a little longer, her face a little paler, her body a little thinner. Voices got a lower, frowns deeper, until there was nothing left to do but to let her rest comfortably.

My dad had run out to the store—mom had wanted pistachios, and any hint of an appetite was cause for immediate celebration. I had been doing homework in the chair beside her bed when the front desk buzzer sounded. I looked up, surprised, because I knew there were no reservations for that day. I looked to my mother, and at the time I only saw her smile, slightly tired but recognizable.

Now I know that the smile hid what was in her eyes. When I think about it, it feels like a punch to the gut.

She motioned with one hand weakly. "Go ahead. I'll be fine."

I made my way out of our quarters and down towards the lobby. I slipped into the office from the door in the hall because "Customers should be greeted from behind the desk" or so my dad always said. As I crossed the office I passed the key board where the only keys hanging were for rooms five and nine. I paused and almost without realizing it, I reached up and pulled the nine key down. The metal felt too warm in my hand.

My mother had told me that I would recognize the special customer for whom we held room nine on reserve. She was right; as I stepped out of the office, he was standing behind the desk. I don't know what I saw or how I recognized him but I knew it was him. I held out the key; he didn't reach for it but took it all the same.

And then, though they were not the words that were running through my head, I heard myself say, "She's in her room in the back."

He nodded without nodding and was gone without going. I stood still for a long moment, staring at the empty space where he had been. My feet began to move and I found myself walking out of the lobby and, hesitating only briefly, turning left. The hallway felt longer than I remembered.

At the end, the door to room nine was slightly ajar. I gently pushed it open further. For a moment there was a sense of movement and a brightening. I exhaled and saw the faint wisps of my own breath. The room was empty save for the faint hint of my mother's scent, from the lotion she always worked into her hands.

I went back to our quarters but sat outside in the hall, not wanting to go inside and see what I already knew. When my father came back he hurried inside, dropping the grocery bag on the floor beside me. I stared at it until his boots came into view once more. He set his back against the wall and slid down next to me. I set my head against his heart and listened as his sobs echoed my own.

I wonder how many room nines there are. How many others keep a bed for a traveler that never sleeps? How many offer a token of comfort to one that never comforts?

I wanted to be angry; I tried to find it buried underneath the seemingly never ending press of grief. But every time I got close, I remembered the look in my mother's eyes, the hitch of pain in her breath, and the lingering sound that had whispered in room nine.

Goodbye.

Mortal Coil

Nicole DeGennaro

The rhythm of the bellows consumed her. The steady pump of her arms, the drip of sweat from her face, the happy glow of the fire—it composed her ideal state, one she eagerly slipped into each day. Her terracotta skin reflected this singular focus on her work, almost every inch pockmarked by sparks or cinders rocketing around during her years of blacksmithing; in that way, she has given a piece of herself to everything she has made, and it has left its mark upon her.

A clear ringing cut through the wheeze of the bellows, pulling her back to the present. When it rang again, she recognized it as a customer using the small iron anvil and hammer on the counter to summon her. She had shaped the iron herself precisely for that purpose, with a sound she would hear over all else in the forge. She motioned to her new apprentice, Wafai, who had been observing her technique.

"Take over," she instructed. Her perfectionist heart hated to leave him unattended. But her practical mind knew the fire would be fine, and practice would lead to mastery.

She wiped her hands on her leather apron, although it mostly transferred more grit onto her skin. Nothing in the smithy had been clean in ages.

"Yessir?" she said by way of greeting, the tail end of the question trailing off as she took in the full sight of the man. She couldn't decide why, but he unsettled her; something about his clothing, his fair skin, his posture, how he stood so still, stone still. It all marked him as other—not just from another region but possibly another country. Everyone from her town was always moving, doing, surviving. The man waited as if he had more time than she could fathom. Patient as a mountain.

"You are the blacksmith Hiba?" he asked. She nodded, words still failing. "You forged the sword that only slays the wicked." It was not a question, but she answered it as if it were.

"Aye." The heat hid the color rising in her face. The sword had become legendary, had secured her reputation and her business. But in truth, she did not remember its creation. She recalled heating the steel, starting to shape it, but the actual forming and finishing faded to a stretch of nothingness in her mind. One morning she woke with the sword waiting for her on the slab and a client she couldn't picture left speechless with satisfaction.

"Indeed you did," he said, as if sensing her thoughts. He spoke her language, but in a strange way. She had never heard the words in the order he chose with the emphasis he used. "It's impressive you've managed so well here, given your gender. But the truly gifted always find a way." People in the region also avoided being so forthright, but that, she appreciated. He had hit a deep, true understanding of her situation on his first strike, and she respected such precise aim.

"I've worked twice as hard to be considered half as good as other smithies."

He chuckled and nodded. Her shoulders relaxed a bit, and only then did she realize how tense she had been.

"I'm glad I found you," he said, leaning on the large stone slab of the counter. She wanted to warn him that his thawb would be stained that way, but she had to admit to herself that both the cut and the fabric of his clothes were unfamiliar. Before his otherness unsettled her again, he continued.

"I need you to create a key."

Business talk, she could handle.

"Should be easy. What kind?"

"The Skeleton Key." She waited for him to elaborate; instead he stared back at her, and she fidgeted in the face of his stillness. When he said nothing more, she frowned, her skin pulling tight across her face from the dry heat in her shop.

"A skeleton key?"

"No. You heard me correctly."

She had. But his request, like his first impression, left her uneasy. Again, she couldn't pinpoint the cause. It would be a simple task; perhaps she could assign it to Wafai. The wrongness of the thought hit her as soon as she had it. Whatever this man wanted, she had to create herself.

"I don't think I can help you." Her voice sounded cold, hollow: the antithesis of her environment. She did not believe in superstition, but she did not want to ignore her instinct to be wary.

"On the contrary. Only you can help me. Only someone who could forge the hammer held by the worthy, and the trident that tames the sea, and the scales that seal the fate of the dead—all that, and more— only that person can create this."

A buzzing filled her head, stifled her breath. It was as if he had called her by many different names that were all somehow her own. His words had untethered something within her, and she scrambled to anchor it again.

You have me confused with someone else, she wanted to say.

"What type of lock is this key meant to open?" The question came from her sideways, sidled in front of the words she had intended to say and snuck out while she recuperated from her disorientation. Talking about the project as if she would take it on settled her stomach, moored her back to reality. The man had not shifted once during their entire conversation; he would wait forever for her to accept the task.

"Not a type of lock. A type of space."

She shook her head. "That's not possible."

He gave her a knowing smile, and for a moment she thought she recognized the man, the conversation, the expression: *You say that every time.*

"Hiba! The fire's dying," Wafai called from the back. Hiba blinked, wondering why she had come to the front of the shop. She remembered someone hitting the anvil to summon her, but no one stood at the counter. She rushed to the back to take over the bellows again. He had been pumping them too fast, smothering the fire instead of nurturing it. She waved him aside.

"Watch; there's a rhythm." She set to it, and with each slow exhale from the device that gently revived the fire, a lingering unease slipped from her mind.

She sat at her work table, sketching with vigor as the early morning sun peeked in through the window. A beam caught her in the eyes, pulling her from her reverie. She couldn't remember if she had gone to bed the previous night. When she glanced down, charcoal dust was smeared across her hands, and sketch after frenzied sketch showed key after bizarre key. Most had been scribbled out into near obscurity, deemed unfit by her subconscious.

She sighed, resigning herself to cleaning up the parchment scraps and preparing the shop for business. Something so easy should not be consuming so much of her time. And what did she want with such a thing anyway? The idea must have seized her at some point, but she could not recall when. Typically she chose more complicated personal projects. Simple or not, it would have to wait until she and Wafai finished the paying jobs.

"Hiba?"

She started and turned. Wafai stood a few feet away, brow furrowed in concern as he tied his apron around his waist. The sun was sliding away from the confines of the window, meaning about an hour had passed since she had intended to stoke the fire and begin the day in her shop. Instead, a dozen more crumpled sketches surrounded her, all depicting the key that haunted her mind.

She did not believe in superstition, but she did not want to ignore such a persistent urge. With a sweep of her arm she cleared the table and motioned for Wafai to approach. She would put him in charge of all the paying jobs, under her guidance. That would give her enough free time to continue considering her current obsession. Wafai's sidelong glances followed her around the shop, but he said nothing about her preoccupied state.

After she set him up at the larger forge, she started a fire in the smaller one. She had installed two when she had first opened her shop, her optimism getting the better of her. But even with her reputation, she rarely had enough work to justify lighting both.

She hadn't been able to sketch the item, so she decided to try and find it in the iron, which she could often manage. After all, she had chosen to be a blacksmith and not an artist for a reason. As she heated a rod, she closed her eyes and envisioned a key that could open a certain type of room. She paused, unsure why that would be the requirement that would come to mind. It certainly made the task more challenging. The practical voice in her head told her that such an object couldn't exist, but she silenced it and instead let her heart guide her imagination. She thought of rooms with similar layouts, but discarded the idea. The key would need to respond to something not easily altered or removed; with that settled, she landed on the idea of rooms with the same mural: a knight battling a dragon.

Holding the idea in her mind, she opened her eyes and set to work: pounding, tapering, reheating, shaping, refining. But the closer she got to completion, the more she sensed its wrongness, as if the universe itself wanted her to stop wasting her time. Something in her gut led her to push on, to ignore the outside force that whispered to her to move on to her next attempt.

She focused on the imagined mural, adding more and more detail. The knight injured, the sand around him spotted red. The dragon rearing, furious, the knight's spear in its side. No clear victor, the battle forever paused at the halfway point. Each aspect she added to the mural only emphasized her impossible task. How could a key open similar rooms with different locks? How would it know the contents of the room?

She couldn't ignore the logistics, and it became a distraction, throwing off the steadiness of her blows, the rhythm of the bellows.

But she couldn't leave anything unfinished. At the end of the day, she evaluated the result: the bow a stylized dragon head, the blade a shot of flame ejected from the dragon's mouth, and the teeth as blunted tendrils of fire. She had crafted a fierce but useless object—a key that instead of opening many rooms would open none.

"May I see it?"

A strange man was waiting for her when she opened the shop the next morning. Something about him unsettled her, although she couldn't say why. It might have been his moon-pale skin, his slate-gray clothing, his stiff posture.

"See what?" she asked as she stepped aside to let him into the shop. Keeping her eyes off him put her at ease.

"Ah, of course," he said, giving her a terrible sense that they had had a similar conversation many times—too many times. "The key."

She wanted to ask how he knew about it but feared the answer. So she told herself Wafai must have mentioned it around town or to his family, and word had spread. The simplicity of such an answer appealed to her, especially in light of the complicated feelings the strange man evoked.

15

"Why do you want to see it?" she asked, intending to refuse. Instead, before he could answer she moved into the back and returned holding the item.

"Who wouldn't want to see such a thing?"

"Not much interest in a key to nothing."

"Oh, it's a key to something," he said as she handed it to him. He ran his hands along its curves, turned it over and over. "An impressive attempt, albeit not what I requested."

She remembered the man then; their previous conversation hit her mind in one solid strike that rang in her skull. "I know."

"But it's served its own purpose." He smiled, and she struggled to interpret it as encouraging or mischievous. "I didn't expect you to succeed on the first try. This kind of craftsmanship takes time. And I have plenty of that."

Hiba could not make sense of the man. He set her on edge but also comforted some more distant part of her. She couldn't choose which feeling to trust.

"But it can't take forever—if you didn't need it, you wouldn't have asked for it," she reasoned.

"If only things were that straightforward. Most things we ask for, we don't need. Some would say the universe does not need this object, but more powerful forces believe it does. I think once you make it, you'll understand. And it won't take you forever. It never does."

He tipped his strange hat to her as he pocketed the item. She didn't try to stop him as he left; her gut told her it belonged to him.

Three more days wasted on her impossible project. She entertained the idea of moving away, taking up farming out of spite. Wafai kept the shop going; Hiba could only focus on keys. She studied every one she could find, as if they could unlock the secret of creating the one she needed. Again she forged with ideas of ones that could open rooms with no windows, rooms that were all the first one the left in any building, rooms that had doors made of wood from the same source. Each attempt resulted in nothing more than a decoration, a simulacrum.

The man did not return to see these failures, which contributed to her frustration; his absence confirmed her suspicions of their uselessness. She didn't need his encouragement, she told herself, or the distracting discomfort of his presence. But she worried that her first try had been her best, and each subsequent attempt brought her further from the Skeleton Key.

The day she decided on her fourth variation, humidity turned the air to sludge before more than a few daylight hours had passed. The heat in her shop became almost unbearable by midday, but Hiba could not stop envisioning key after key.

"The butcher closed for the day," Wafai said when he returned from his break, his face more red than brown and slick with sweat that refused to evaporate or be wiped away. He swayed on his feet but steadied himself against the table. Hiba glanced out the window, but nothing hinted at an impending relieving rainstorm. She turned back to Wafai, her decision made.

"Go home," she ordered. "We're not going to be getting any business today."

Relief transformed his body language—for a moment, she thought he would float away. He took off his apron and hung it by the door, then paused and looked back at her.

"You'll go home too, yes?"

She nodded, already bending over the table again, sketching. "I just have to finish one thing." After a moment she sensed eyes watching and expected to see the strange man when she glanced up. Instead her gaze met Wafai's, who lingered with a frown. She waved him away.

Once he left, although she practically had to chase him out, she locked the doors, grabbed an iron rod, and began to work.

Her head hummed from the heat; her sweat-slick hands struggled to function. She wheezed as loud as the bellows, the air liquid thick. Laboring alone in such conditions was dangerous, but the noise in her head had developed into a rhythm that yearned to be molded in metal.

The Skeleton Key. The buzz in her head wrapped around the idea.

It doesn't open a *room*. It opens a *space*.

The thought came from nowhere, and she peered into the fire, as if it had whispered to her.

All this time she had imagined a literal room, but a space did not have to be a room. It seemed obvious now, even if her practical mind knew it didn't make a difference. A key could certainly not open a space that was not a room. But somehow the difference in terminology clicked for her in a deeper place where logic could not interfere.

The iron rod glowed a dangerous orange as images began to flash in her head. She stood at the small forge, her breath heavy and her body slow, but she also stood at infinite forges, crafting infinite keys across infinite times. Her arm vibrated with every hammer strike she had ever made and would ever make; the fingers of all her hands curved the cooling iron in ways she had never done before and had always done.

A skeletal hand overlapped all of hers, passing through the skin to rest against her bones. It assisted her, helped shape the object into its essential form. She recognized the hand and its owner as it worked, as she worked, and indeed she believed the universe would be better off without the Skeleton Key. But the hand that overlaid hers had domain over everything and had deemed it necessary.

Her laboring revealed the nature of the space the key would unlock, how it existed in some form in every time, every universe. What she created would open every iteration, reserve the sacred space for the one true unstoppable force. Its manifestations in the mortal realm had to be innocuous, an object of power that appeared mundane, while the uninvited guest would keep its true form close to open the space at will.

She understood all of this as if the iron had revealed it, and the information distracted her from the impossible contortions of her hands as they shaped the iron in unfathomable ways. As she continued, something began burning deep within her, as if someone had stuck a fire-hot iron down her throat until it hit her core. She cried out and tried to retreat from the fire, but she could not escape.

"That's enough," a gentle voice said—not her own, and not the skeleton's. But the work and the incomprehensible pain continued.

"That's enough! You have what you need!"

The skeletal hand vanished, and the infinities collapsed back onto themselves until she stood, shaking, as her one self at her small forge. Then she, too, collapsed.

•••

18

"—assure you," a familiar but distant voice said. "She just needs more rest."

A dry cough forced itself from Hiba's chest, parting her parched lips. A door closed. Footsteps approached, and a cool cloth covered her forehead. She sighed in relief. Cold water followed, the metal of the cup almost sticking to her lips as she drank. Only then did she have the energy to open her eyes.

"You have a determined apprentice there," the man said. He didn't seem so strange anymore—she understood his clothing came from another era, that despite appearances they were meeting outside the human concept of time and place. "He hasn't stopped harassing me about your wellbeing. It's quite obnoxious." He paused. "But endearing too, I suppose."

Hiba groaned, unable to focus on words long enough to reply in full sentences. She wanted to make sense of what had led to her collapse. A fog had been burned away from her mind, and she could recall forging the key—and the sword, the hammer, and so many other legendary objects. In every instance the man in the slate suit had made the request and nursed her to health again after. In every instance, some other force had been involved in the process, her striking hand assisted by another. Her brow furrowed.

When she looked at the man, something shifted in his eyes, as if a painful burning had been doused within him: the relief of recognition.

"Ah, you remember this time." He patted the pocket in which he had placed her first key and gave her a fond smile. She couldn't decide if he was the dragon and she the knight, or the other way around.

"But what am I remembering?" For the first time, she did not get the sense that she had had this conversation with him before. He removed the cloth from her forehead and replaced it with another.

"Being a tool, in one way. Being a force of nature, in another. The interpretation depends on your mood. You have a specific confluence of skills that put you in high demand with—"

She waved at him to stop. The more he explained, the more she realized the knowledge had come back to her along with her memories—and the more she felt his words minimized something monumental.

"Who are you?" She hadn't yet pieced him together. He grinned and removed the second cloth as she sat up.

"Ah, you know," he said. "I make men—and women—wise. I heal wounds. I have close ties with all your clients, but the most recent one in particular."

She understood, but she could not examine that understanding close enough to give the man a name; madness lurked down that route. So she accepted the information without the label.

"I suppose the key is already gone," she said. It was not a question, but he answered it as if it were.

"A creator earns the right to see their work." He smiled. "And I think this is your finest yet." He stood and went to the window in her small bedroom, retrieving an item from the sill. It looked nothing like a key, and perhaps that was the point. It did not belong to her realm, and thus it did not need to adhere to the laws of her universe.

He brought it to her and placed it in her outstretched hands. It fit almost perfectly in one of her palms up to the top knuckles, so she could just curl the tips of her fingers over its rounded edges. Its flat bottom sat warm against her skin, and the rest of its surface twisted in an elaborate knot with no beginning or end. An infinite coil. The longer she held it, the warmer it became, and her bones began to thrum with a vibration that originated from the metal.

It weighed far more than she had anticipated, more than one iron rod would account for. But something else had been added, despite appearances. The burning in her core had been a distraction, a side effect of extracting the additional element—some essential part of her, necessary for this object but no other. She glanced at the man, and he nodded. That small component accounted for the immense weight, just as it gave her life its heft. And the man had intervened to keep the uninvited guest from taking more than it needed.

She gave the item back to him, and he held it out to the room. A skeletal hand reached from the ether and clasped it. A breeze stirred in the room, like a contented sigh coming from the universe itself.

Then the hand and the key vanished.

Vacation
(all I ever wanted)

Kaitlyn Sudol

I t's a nice hotel. Nicer than she would usually bother with. There's a balcony that looks over the pool. There's a view of the ocean. There's a little kitchen and sitting area. There's a minibar.

She spared no expense. She's not going to let some rando ruin it all for her.

"I'm on vacation," she insists to him. "It's a vacation it's—I'm off, I'm chilling out, I'm not working for the first time in a lifetime, okay?"

"I know," the guy says. Black slacks, black shirt, black blazer, all offsetting his pale, pale skin—the opposite of her, all dark skin swathed in a gauzy white sundress she bought specifically for this trip. He looks like he belongs at a funeral, not a tropical resort. "But vacation doesn't stop death."

"Yes," she tells him. "Yes, it definitely does."

They're sitting in the little lounge area of her suite. He's got his knees together, his hands folded neatly on top of them, sitting with his back ramrod straight, eyes boring into her. He's been that way since she got here and collapsed onto the arm chair across from him. She knew what it meant then. That doesn't mean she has to agree with or go along with it.

She gets up from the chair and paces around the suite. It's so nice. It's *so* nice. Her first real vacation since she started this stupid job. She's been looking forward to it with unparalleled enthusiasm.

"The world keeps spinning," the guy says. "And some things are inescapable."

"Only if you resign yourself to that fact," she says. "Let's give a big ol' 'fuck you' to fate. Let's just . . . ignore this and keep going. Let's show the universe who's boss."

The guy is unswayed by her pleading. He's still sitting there, calm as anything. Serene, even. She wants to punch him in his placid, composed face.

"I'm secure in my fate," the guy says. "I'm aware of my destiny. I have no desire to buck it."

"Well bully for you," she snaps. She runs her hands through her hair and stares balefully out at the pool. It looks like something out of a movie, beautiful and blue. She can hear the ocean crashing. She can smell a hint of salt in the air, even though the sliding glass doors are closed, even though the air conditioning is on.

She gestures sharply out the window, glaring at him.

"Look at that!" she says. "Look at that beautiful shoreline! Look at that pool! There's a bar floating in the pool! There's a bar that you can swim up to right there in the pool! Look at the sun, at the clouds—look at the palm trees! This place is beautiful. It's the stuff dream vacations are made of. Why don't we just put it off? Don't you want to go out and enjoy this day, this place? Don't you want a vacation?"

The man still hasn't moved and looks thoroughly unimpressed by her pleading. He's a dark stain on her perfect hotel room, a dirty smudge in a sea of soft white linens and light wood furniture. He doesn't look like the sort of guy who would be tempted by the idea of surf lessons and fruity drinks and sunbathing, but she has to try.

"I don't need a vacation," he says. "I don't want to put this off. I know what needs to happen, and I'd rather just get it over with, if it's all the same to you."

"It's *not* all the same to me!" she insists. "Jesus, man—you don't understand! You don't get it! I work nonstop! I never get a break, a rest, a reprieve. That's all I want—a weekend, a *day* to myself. A day to relax. A day to stop worrying for once in my life that the world is going to end without me."

She's so sick and tired of carrying so much on her shoulders. It's weighing her down—she has a literal crick in her neck that's been lingering for ages and no amount of hot water soaks or massage can drive it away. It took so long to set this up—to find coverage, to train her substitutes, to get all the right approvals and sign-offs before she could even book the hotel room. And the last week—getting ready to go, preparing her replacements, crossing off everything from her to-do list; it was a month's worth of work crammed into just seven endless days. It was a nightmare made bearable by the carrot on the stick, by the pictures of this room pinned to her wall, by the pictures of the view.

She wants to cry. The man in front of her is unmoved.

"You don't understand," she says. "You just—" She slumps forward. There's nothing else for it. She can tell by his face, by his posture, by the set of his shoulders. She can't sway him. And if she tries to ignore him, he'll just follow her. She can already tell. A black cloud over her supposedly relaxing holiday.

"I'm supposed to be on *vacation*," she says one last time. She's mournful. It's fitting.

"Things change," he says. "I'm ready now. It has to be now." His expression flickers for just a moment. There's just a hint of pity there. "I'm sorry, if it's any consolation."

"It's not," she lies, straightening up. "Okay. If this is gonna happen, it's gonna happen." She ties her hair back, the snap of the elastic echoing in the room. "If this is gonna happen, it means transport and paperwork and filing. The sooner we start, the sooner it's over, right?"

The man blinks at her slowly.

"You would know better than I would," he says.

If she starts now, maybe she can salvage the last half of her vacation.

She pulls out her phone and turns it on, waiting for it to power up, waiting for it to find a connection, waiting for her stupid work app to send her all the details.

The messages come through first.

D, I'm sorry, but I need you to . . .

I know you're on vacation but . . .

It's right at your hotel so it makes sense . . .

She ignores them and taps the blinking icon. A picture of the guy pops up on her screen.

"Mr. Bartholomew Trent," she says, her voice flat. "Seventy-six. Heart attack." She glances up at him. "Are you sure you want to do this? Seventy-six is really young and I'm sure I can—"

"I'm sure," Mr. Trent says.

She sighs and takes one last look out at the beautiful ocean, the idyllic poolside.

"Okay, Mr. Trent," she says, and holds out her hand. "Let's get you to the afterlife."

She'd better be paid overtime for this. It's just not fair—even Death deserves a damn vacation.

Memory

Lara Eckener

Time moves as the hawks fly
  their nests hanging empty in the night
  overcome by magic or insomnia
the rustling of their wings
puts us down to rest, and even without sleep
the birds do still call in the mornings
to wake we travelers
from the corpse born dreams we search
—for the poems that will remain unread,
for the art in the monuments
whose locations will never be mapped,
for the forests clinging to the mountainsides
none of us will ever climb—
and in our sunrise sorrows
we mistake this vast and lonely beauty
as desire's dying breath.
But without us light will fall
on the fields in the morning
and the midnight nests will collect their kin
just as the faces of the flowers
follow the sun, and the leaves of the trees
turn up to catch the glow from the moon.
Compelled, a long walk will lead us
to another abandoned home
with drowsy curtains fluttering in disused windows
and a conclusion as inevitable as rest:
no room is ever empty
if it contains
the final hopes of one well-lived.

Part II

Power

1. The ability to do something or act in a particular way, especially as a faculty or quality.

2. The capacity or ability to direct or influence the behavior of others or the course of events.

Return to Form

Nicole DeGennaro

J ames knocked on the digiglass separating him from the clerk; Sylvia, according to her holotag. The ad display—*Explore the new frontier! Apply today*—flickered for a moment. But considering that he had been able to walk right up to the counter, it seemed not many people were eager to be colonizers. He hoped that might work in his favor. A few other applicants sat in the waiting area finishing their paperwork—using old-fashioned printed forms, even with all the technology embedded in almost every available surface. The government still loved its literal paper trail.

"I want to appeal," he said. He brandished his denied form, which had been stamped by the reviewer on the top page. "I went to school with someone named Chris Belasco. I think he's biased."

One of the other applicants coughed, and James glanced over. All three had looked up at the agitation in his voice, but none of them would make eye contact. The older couple hunched back over their papers, and the pale man coughed again. It sounded just as fake as the first one. His husband patted his back with a gentle umber hand.

The third person, a woman about James' age, regarded him briefly with her piercing blue eyes before turning away. He glanced down at his application. REJECTED. It stared up at him in big red letters.

When he faced the counter again, Sylvia had finally turned her attention away from her work screen and toward him. The ad had disappeared, so he looked her straight in the eye as he glared and slid his papers through the slot. In addition to receiving live updates on his status in the queue via holocard, the government had kindly also sent a fucking letter. REJECTED.

She took the application and frowned as she glanced at it, although the genetic scanner in the doorway had already taken care of identifying him. Then it had sent his information to all the employees' work screens. She tucked a loose strand of her black hair, so shiny it seemed metallic, behind her ear. Then she passed James' papers under a thin, elevated pane of glass to her left. He had never seen that tech before, unlike the old ubiquitous genetic scanner. He strained to watch through the digiglass. It obscured anything viewed at an angle, so he could only see Sylvia clearly. The glass pane, resting parallel to the counter, revealed more red lettering on his application, although he couldn't read it. His stomach dropped.

"I'm sorry, Mr. Felder, but you can't appeal this denial. It's your second in six months; now you have a year-long waiting period." Something about her tone—placating but dismissive—told him his waiting period would end up being forever. He would never be approved.

"Yeah, that's to apply again, *Sylvia*," James nearly spat. "But I want to appeal *this* application. Belasco's a jackass! He's probably mad about some dumb high school prank." James' palms started to sweat. He peered around at the other applicants, hoping one of them might help him convince this woman to put his appeal through. But they all kept their eyes elsewhere. He could practically hear them wishing he would accept the verdict and move on. They didn't understand the importance.

"Sir, this Chris Belasco is a woman." Sylvia gave him a pointed look. James swallowed and gripped the counter. "And all our reviewers are carefully vetted. They cannot evaluate forms from people they may know." She slid his papers back to him. Her words sent his mind into a freefall, and he began scrabbling for any feasible handhold to grasp. He had made a promise, had sworn this would work. He couldn't go home a liar, a failure.

"No—but—I have to get to Mars." The feeble words stammered out of his dry throat before he could stop them. He snatched his application from under her fingers, as if he were stealing something precious from her instead of taking back proof of his worthless life. REJECTED. The large red letters caught his eye even as he tried to focus on Sylvia. "You don't understand. *You don't understand.* I have to get to Mars."

"You've reached your limit, Mr. Felder. I'm sorry. You have to wait a year."

He stared at the woman through the digiglass for a moment. Then he lunged forward, slamming both palms against the barrier. REJECTED. REJECTED. The word pulsed in his mind, and he pounded his hands against the divider again. The impact shook through his arms up to his elbows, chased by little darts of pain. Sylvia didn't flinch. A warning flashed across the digiglass: Please step back and calm down or security will intervene.

"I promised her! I promised I'd get her to Mars. I can't fail her. I can't!" James yelled, still slamming his hands against the barrier until his fingers numbed and his palms reddened. "Please. PLEASE!" The screen continued flashing its warning, unheeded.

"Whoever she is, sir, she'd need to apply for herself," Sylvia said. James wound up for another strike against the glass when someone grabbed his arms from behind. He strained to see over his shoulder, ready to fight off the interloper. Two security guards had appeared, and one twisted James' arms behind his back until he winced. Still, he struggled.

"Sir, if you don't stop we'll have to arrest you," the taller of the two guards said. After one last thrash, James went limp and hung his head. His eyes fell back to his application as tears blurred his vision. Would she understand that he had tried, that he had tried so hard to get her where she needed to be?

The older man coughed again, and James whipped around to face him.

"Thanks for your help, assholes," James spat. The couple gaped at him as if he were crazy; the woman stared as if he were a sideshow.

The guard holding him turned him toward the exit as the taller one grabbed his papers from the counter and shoved them into James' right hand. Then they forced him out the door of the Emigration Center; when they released him he stumbled down the steps and sank to his knees on the sidewalk instead of saving himself the fall.

"Fucking weirdos," the tall guard muttered as he closed the door behind James. They would blacklist him now, just like the bank had; the genetic scanner would bar him from entering the building. REJECTED. The word burned in his brain, morphed his shame back into anger. He tore his application in half, then began ripping it into smaller pieces.

"Hey, you all right?" someone asked; a firm hand on James' shoulder froze him in mid-tear. He turned and looked up at the second security guard, the shorter, younger one who had been grasping his arms. James rose to his feet without answering.

"Mars will be there for a while. You'll get another chance," she said, giving him an amicable smile. He didn't bother reading her holotag. Instead, he finished tearing his application, then threw the pieces in her face and walked away.

He stood outside the bedroom door. He hadn't turned on the hall light, and he wanted to believe the darkness hid him, but he knew she had sensed his presence. She always did. Still, he couldn't bring himself to knock and enter the room. If he could stand in the unlit hallway forever, he wouldn't have to face her disappointment, her anger—he wouldn't have to admit he was a failure.

Just then a soft light slipped under the door and illuminated his socked feet. She was beckoning to him. James allowed himself one more moment in the hallway, in the world where nothing had yet changed between them. Then he knocked. After a few seconds, the light pulsed once. James opened the door and stepped into the bedroom, leaving the darkness for her gentle light.

He couldn't look at her; he couldn't speak even when she asked him what had happened. So he turned and closed the door, as if that would disconnect him from his past. When he faced her again, he could sense her agitation; it generated heat in the room. Instead of waiting for him to speak, she summoned the information from him as she always could, pulling it from his throat.

"I'm sorry," he said, gagging on the words as she drew them out. "They rejected me. I can't apply again for a year." He coughed and followed the deep scratches in the wooden floor of her bedroom, tracing them with his eyes up to the legs of the bed on which she rested. But he dared not let his gaze wander further.

"I don't know!" he said when she asked why, his words a defensive shout. "I tried. I begged! I told them—I told them we have to get to Mars. They don't care." She cut him off, and he hunched his shoulders, bracing against her anger. His hair began to stand on end, as if he had goosebumps. But he didn't. He rubbed his arms, wincing at a shock of static electricity.

"They want good people; I'm not a good person." Again she drew the words from him, although he had added the annoyance in his tone.

"So unless you can erase my past, we're stuck here. Probably forever!" Since he had met her, he had spent many moments wondering why she had chosen him when she could have had anybody, and the application rejection made his inadequacy undeniable. But he dared not ask her why; he dreaded her answer.

REJECTED. The word had ingrained itself within him. He turned to leave, wanting to rush out of the room, out of the house even. But a few soothing words from her stopped him halfway to the door. He ran a shaking hand through his hair once, twice, then covered his eyes with the same hand as he held back tears. She apologized, as if his failures were her fault.

She turned off her light, and he faced her once more, his hand falling to his side. He could look at her now, take in the curves of her silhouette outlined by the low light filtering in through the curtains.

"No, no. Don't apologize. I'm just frustrated. I hate letting you down." He went as close to her as he dared, stopping about a foot away, but he avoided touching her—it would be too painful, too dangerous.

"I don't know what else to do. Tell me what to do."

After a few more gentle words, she told James her new plan. He frowned when she finished and took a step back, hoping to see her more clearly in the fading light.

"You're sure that will work? That will get us to Mars?"

She replied in the affirmative.

"Then yes, of course. I've let you down so much, how could I say no?"

She beckoned him closer, told him not to turn away. Warned him it would be excruciating.

James stood his ground and kept his arms by his sides. No resistance. The idea that he had one last shot to help her, to get her where she needed to be, soothed the scars from his mistakes. She would push him beyond all that.

She turned her light back on, starting with a low, warm glow that reminded him of how faint she had been when she had called to him in the forest all those years ago. He had nurtured her as best he could but hadn't been able to complete his most recent task. Until now, he hoped. Her brightness intensified, and James squinted but kept his gaze steady. Her colors were even more beautiful than he remembered, a rainbow halo of gas swirling around a hot, solid core that glowed with brilliant light, as if a swatch of the universe's fabric had fallen from its rightful place and ended up in his possession. But he had never controlled her—he had always been her unfit servant.

Soon she shone so bright and hot that her gaseous halo evaporated, and James' eyes began to water. The tip of his nose started to burn, and he did his best not to cry out, but she hadn't finished yet; she expanded to fill the room, blinding him, melting his clothes and skin until he succumbed to the pain, to her power.

Someone slid an application through the slit at the bottom of the digiglass barrier. Sylvia Lu glanced up.

"Do you have any questions?" she asked the woman. The reverberation of her voice sounded different than normal; instead of the echo bouncing back to her after passing through the microphone in the divider, the words fell flat from her lips, as if she had spoken into a pillow. She almost repeated herself, worried the microphone had stopped working, when the woman replied.

"Should I?"

Sylvia suppressed a frown at the woman's tone—it came across as a sneer, but her body language didn't corroborate that interpretation. Sylvia glanced at the first page of the form. Janice Felder.

"Hm. We just had a man with the same last name come in a few days ago. Are you related to a James Felder?" she asked.

"No relation," Janice said, offering an unsettling smile that seemed more like she was baring her teeth. Sylvia looked away and flipped through the paperwork for any glaring errors. Then she slid it under the digiscanner, which would label it with a genecode from the door scanner and flag its place in the queue for reviewers. But nothing happened. Sylvia sighed and tried again.

"That's just as well; I think that guy was a little off-kilter," she said as she kept trying. "They might blacklist his whole family just in case it's a genetic thing." She gave up, instead initialing the application in the designated box and adding it to that day's pile. Then she scribbled the application number on a small index card—normally it would all be on a holocard, when the technology worked the way it should.

"You can't be too careful when you're colonizing a planet!" Sylvia smiled and slid the card to Janice through the divider.

Instead of returning the smile, something flashed in Janice's eyes, a supernovic threat of violence, and Sylvia quickly pulled her hand back from the barrier. But again everything else about Janice—from her relaxed posture to her delicate features—contradicted Sylvia's unease.

"Anyway," she continued after a pause. The hand she had withdrawn was hovering by the button to call security; she forced it to relax into her lap. "Your paperwork looks fine, so it'll be sent to processing later today. You should hear back in a few weeks."

Janice frowned and placed both her palms on the counter, leaning close to the divider. She moved slowly, as if she had all of time to complete the one action. She gazed hard at Sylvia, her frown somehow as aggressive as her posture. Sylvia slid her chair back a few inches.

"It takes that long?" Janice asked, her voice butter smooth. Then she muttered something else that almost sounded like "Humans are so inefficient," but Sylvia didn't dare ask her to repeat herself. Despite her average height and build, the woman had an imposing presence, as if just under her midnight skin lurked a massive and powerful predator.

Again something flashed in Janice's eyes, and then Sylvia heard herself saying,

"I can put a rush on it, Ms. Felder. That way you'd hear back in three to five days." Sylvia blinked when she finished speaking and rubbed her sore throat. She coughed, then bit her lip. She couldn't remember the specific reason Janice needed an expedited review of her application, but she did recall it being valid. Had it been a sick relative on Mars? Something about her job? Sylvia absently pulled the form from the pile and checked the appropriate areas to rush the process.

"I suppose that will have to suffice," Janice said, and the deep disappointment in her voice almost elicited an apology from Sylvia. Janice turned and walked away; the minute she exited the door, the sounds of the other tellers and customers rushed in to fill the vacuum her presence had created. Sylvia flinched at the noise—not because of its volume, but because she hadn't noticed its absence until it had returned. She sat stunned for a few seconds as her ears adjusted to the normal sounds of her work environment, and after another few moments she couldn't remember what had shocked her in the first place.

She had been helping someone, but she couldn't recall anything about the person. When she tried, her mind could only grasp the image of a brilliant burning light too intense to be viewed head on.

"Next!" she called, her voice booming through the microphone that she had forgotten about and echoing back to her. As the next applicant approached her window, Sylvia noticed two hand prints burned onto the pale granite surface of the counter.

Janice Felder—what terribly bland names most humans had—got word of her application approval two days after she had dropped it off with Sylvia Lu. Her shuttle to Mars left in a few days, at the end of the week.

She had spent much of her time since dropping off her paperwork pulling strings in the minds of the Emigration Center workers who came into contact with her form to get it pushed through the old-fashioned way, with as little technology involved as possible. After all, she wouldn't appear in any of the government databases. Minds she could easily fool—technology took more finesse. So she disabled it instead, and she had put her application at the top of every pile along the way. Humans might not mind waiting, as essentially their whole lives were spent waiting to die and nothing more, but Janice had been inactive long enough—by a measure of time that humans could not even fathom. She no longer had patience for delays.

The more she had to think of herself as Janice, the more she liked the temporary façade. It couldn't compare to her true state or the glory of her real name, which would roughly translate to the human concept of immolation, but it had its own appeal. No doubt some of the sentimentality came from the remnants of James' consciousness still floating among her other assimilated energy. Fragments of every being she had absorbed over the eons lingered within her, although their prominence faded over time. All of them deserved to see what she would accomplish thanks to their sacrifice, and James most of all. He had done a great deal for her over the years, even if he had ultimately been inadequate.

He must have been shocked by her past, though—he had thought his petty, small-scale existence had made him "not a good person"—and maybe that was true by human standards. But Janice and her kind operated on a different set of morals applied on a larger scale. Humans would likely call her a monster, and she kept expecting James' remaining consciousness to label her as such.

Yet she didn't sense any judgment from him, maybe because she hadn't judged him either. She knew all about struggling to survive, calibrating the measure of right and wrong, sometimes choosing to do things that looked malicious on the surface with the hope of the best outcome. And she, too, had been caught and punished by her kind, as James had been by his. So perhaps instead of seeing her as a monster, he saw her as a kindred spirit. Perhaps it was fitting that they had ended up as one entity.

It had been coincidence and nothing more that led to the fortuitous union. Her punishment for her actions had been exile, and after depleting most of her power, some of her kind had picked a distant planet at random that had seemed to be in an insufficient system, one that didn't have the right kind of energy to allow her to recharge. They thought this fate better than extinguishing her outright.

They had been wrong at every moment. Most importantly, they had underestimated her will to survive.

Her arrival on the planet had been an extinction event. Even in her weakened state, the little planet that would become Earth to its inhabitants had never seen the likes of her. At first, her own arrival had worked against her, as once she regained her bearings after the crash, there had been little left on the planet to help her reenergize. A lesser creature would have let herself dissipate—it would have been faster, easier. But like the few species that clung to life and thrived on Earth in her aftermath, she too had refused to die.

Instead, she waited, found ways to attract what creatures she could to gather energy piecemeal. Heat brought some, light brought others, noise brought others still. It all drained her bit by bit, so she had to weigh the effort. Sometimes she miscalculated; sometimes she succeeded.

And oh, when humans had finally emerged. She had known right away they would be her escape, would help her recover and enjoy her revenge.

She had tried to wait for humans to figure out how to use their latent telepathic powers before she began reaching out, but it became apparent to her that the species had turned its focus to technological and other outward development rather than the internal. Instead, she had to wait until she became strong enough to communicate directly with the human mind in the language of the area, and by then she had hidden herself away deep in what little unblemished forest remained. It took a long time for someone to hear her—even longer for one of those humans to listen instead of ignore. They had changed the Earth by then, altered its composition and energy so it would no longer be useful to her. If she hadn't been in so fragile a state, the alterations wouldn't have mattered. But she needed the right mix of elements to not only return her former power but push it beyond her previous limits.

Now, thanks to James, she had gathered enough energy to become corporeal but not enough to reach Mars on her own. Absorbing him had used a great deal of her energy, and she had needed days to recuperate and hope that last exertion would pay off. It had. James had not failed her after all. And she had done him an unwitting favor as well: she had saved him from the cancer her radiation had inflicted.

Once she had recovered, it had not taken much calculation for her to realize that at this point it would be safer—with some manipulation from her—to follow the humans' inane processes in the penultimate stage of her resurrection. It would take her longer to try and find the type of energy she needed in the sufficient amount to get herself to Mars, and she would risk depleting the power she did have in the process. So instead she would board one of those adorably impractical spaceships.

This choice also benefited humans. Instead of her return to form causing another mass extinction event—one that would obliterate the Earth itself—she would take a planet with far less life on it. A planet that humans wouldn't miss, although they would notice its absence. And she was glad to leave the species alive. After watching humans struggle to survive and evolve over the centuries, she wanted to see how they would continue to develop. Her kind did not often indulge in that sort of affection, but it didn't bother her. Being exiled had made her unlike anything else in the universe.

These thoughts and reminiscences colored her last days on Earth. She didn't have to focus on packing because she didn't need anything but herself and Mars. Still, she sifted through James' few

42

possessions as her mind wandered because it would be suspicious if she showed up without luggage for a one-way trip. She only needed enough stuff so that the bag would appear normal in the scanners. If necessary, she could pull strings in the mind of anyone who questioned her, but each manipulation took energy she didn't want to spare. Better to fit in and save her meager reserves for her final assimilation.

When she finished packing a random collection of James' clothes and possessions that she thought a human might wish to have, including the personal display devices most of them always had on hand, she sat and waited for her remaining time to tick by. Janice did not need to eat or sleep—at least not in ways that resembled how humans performed those tasks—but she went into a stasis to maintain her energy levels. She had beautiful dreams of destruction.

"Musta applied six times in the last ten years," the man behind Janice in line said. At first she thought he was talking to himself. But when she glanced at him, he caught her eye and smiled, and she realized he expected her to participate in the conversation.

"Dunno what changed," he continued. "Maybe they got sicka seein' my name." He guffawed at his own joke. She smiled, and judging from how the man's eyes bugged in response, she still hadn't quite mastered that particular human expression in her illusory form. She couldn't tell the difference between a smile, sneer, and grimace—and it all left such room for interpretation.

She hoped her lack of a verbal reply might deter the man from continuing the conversation, but instead he pressed on.

"Kinda excitin' to be a pioneer, like the old cowboys. Goin' to new frontiers." The man was regurgitating phrases from the Emigration Center ads that plastered every available surface, but she couldn't tell if it had been deliberate. Most things humans did seemed to have little forethought.

The man's inane babble further convinced Janice she had chosen the best option in getting to Mars despite the frustrations along the way. The few thousand humans already on that planet would see an actual new frontier, not something visible from their home planet's sky. When she assimilated Mars, anything living on the planet would be absorbed as well—not dead in the way humans thought of death. In fact, in Janice's opinion, they would be far more alive than their delicate bodies would ever allow. All of them so desperate to go a mere 140 million miles. She would show them parts of the universe unknown to the human race.

She followed her bag as it went through its third content scanner and she her third body scan; it made her wonder what humans so deeply feared in each other that they required so much security yet would still colonize a planet together.

Instead of disabling the technology as she had at the Emigration Center, which would only bring the already slow progress toward the spaceship to a complete halt, she had to manipulate the minds of the workers reading the scanner so her results would seem normal. Otherwise the elaborate, temporary illusion of Janice would appear anomalous—if it appeared at all.

Once she passed through the scanner—the final one, it seemed— she turned her attention back to the people around her. They all sweated in the sunlight, as only the workers had access to shade; many had cloths to wipe their faces, and some poured water on their heads. Janice could not feel the heat or humidity. As with most things at the human scale, she found it negligible. But she played along, adding sweat and increasing the breathing rate for her façade.

"—wife and kids three months ago." The man behind her in line had continued despite her lack of response and attention. In fact all the people around her were chatting; apparently humans enjoyed talking to pass the time.

"They got a little pod or whatever all set up for us." He chuckled. "Goin' from one home to another. Guy can't get luckier than that." They shuffled a few steps forward in the line. "Anyone waitin' for ya on that red planet?"

Everyone. They just don't know it. "No. I'm going for a new start."

"Aw, get outta here. Ya can't be more than 30—what's a woman like you gotta escape from?"

An inadequate prison.

She gave a sly smile, she hoped. "Doesn't matter now; it's all being left behind."

"Fair enough, fair enough." Before their conversation could continue, a guard pointed to the man and waved him toward a blocked-off area to the right of the line. At first Janice thought he had been chosen to skip the line and board the ship, and her agitation flared. The hair of the humans around her began to rise, like it would before a lightning strike, and she forced herself to calm down and keep her energy under control. She couldn't blow her chance now. For a moment she feared she had already passed the tipping point as the air crackled around her. The small talk died down as people glanced around and shifted on their feet. But then as quick as she had lost control, she regained it, pulling her precious energy back into her core. People fixed their hair, rubbed their bare arms. Then they went back to talking.

"Shit. Always happens to me," the man muttered as he followed the guard behind the screen, and she realized he had been selected for a randomized full-body search. So she relished the silence of his absence until the next person tried to engage her attention.

After another half an hour of random, brief conversations with the humans in the line, Janice had her bag back in her hand and stood at the base of the ramp for the space shuttle. She had to suppress her laughter at how humans seemed to pick the most difficult way to do anything; so much unnecessary machinery to make such a short trip. But even with their inadequacies, they found a way. She respected that kind of determination.

Everyone abandoned the orderly nature of the screening lines inside the expanse of the ship, where the passengers sought their assigned seats with no help. Janice worked her way to a mostly empty area and went down the row of five seats to the window, a perk she had manipulated for herself. She wanted to watch the approach to the planet that would be her rebirth.

She stowed her bag in the compartment marked with her seat number and then sat down. More waiting, so much time spent waiting. But it wouldn't be for much longer. More humans boarded the ship until no empty seats remained; Janice took in all the hopeful and nervous faces. She wondered how many of them would still be on the ship if they knew how the trip would end. But humans lived in a constant state of unknowing; that they lived their lives despite such massive blank spots in their knowledge impressed her. She had found much to admire in a species on a planet her kind had disregarded.

To thank them, Janice would show these few hundred humans, plus the few thousand already on Mars, more about the universe than their limited brains would have been able to comprehend on their own. Once they became part of her, though, their current corporeal restrictions would be irrelevant. As they had taught her to see the universe in different ways, so she would return the favor. She anticipated that moment, for them and for her.

Coat Check

Kaitlyn Sudol

It takes Adrian two weeks to pack up everything in the beach house and ship it back up north. It's two long, trying weeks of weeding through his grandparents' belongings, deciding what to spare and what to donate, boxing everything up, and sending it where it needs to go. It's exhausting and he makes sure to let Adelaide know every night when she calls to check in from London.

"You could be here helping with this," he tells her. "You and what's his name."

"You know his name is Franklin, don't front," she says. "And you know how busy we are. It's not my fault Gran left us that moldering old house. You could have just sold it sight-unseen and been done with it."

Yeah, he could have, but the idea of just giving part of his family's history away was like an itch he couldn't scratch for days before he decided to take the time to go down south and clean the place out before putting it on the market. There could have been family treasures inside, mementos from his grandparents' life in Brazil, relics of their past that needed to be preserved.

In the end, it was mostly old clothes that he donated to some thrift shops, way too many old newspapers, and the assorted crap you'd expect in an old beach house. He saved some photos and some of the clothes, emptying trunks and suitcases and laying the contents out on the sand out back to see what was worth holding on to. Books, too, and some kitchen stuff (the cast-iron pans were in *amazing* condition), and by the end of the two weeks he was just shoving things into boxes and sending them north to deal with later. Maybe he'd leave it all in Adelaide's empty apartment, waiting for her when she and her fiancé returned from London. It would serve her right.

He lets that thought keep him awake and aware as he drives home from the post office. The last of the boxes have been sent off, he's bone-tired, and in the morning he'll take one last look around the house, leave the keys for the cleaners, and fly back up to Boston. He's almost done.

Back at the house, he doesn't even make it to the bedroom. He lies down on the couch, just to close his eyes for a second, and passes out before he can even take out his contacts.

Morning comes to Adrian slowly, first in the bird calls outside, then in the sunlight filtering across his face. Right. He fell asleep on the couch last night. He should get up now, take a shower, change his clothes, but moving just seems like a lot of work. It's much easier to lie still and listen to the birds and the ocean and the measured breaths of someone else in the room holy shit—

He sits up abruptly, because apparently he has no sense of self-preservation. The obvious thing to do would be to pretend to be sleeping until he could come up with a plan, but nope, now he's sitting up with wide-eyes, his hands shaking, staring at—

Well, the burglar is very handsome, at least. He's going to be killed by a lean, toned, willowy guy his age who's startlingly beautiful, which shouldn't be a consolation, but it kind of is. At least the last thing he sees will be easy on the eyes.

Except the guy isn't doing anything. He's standing next to the couch, staring down at Adrian, but not speaking or moving. He doesn't have a weapon. He does have eyes that remind Adrian of the ocean and soft brown hair that looks like it has silver highlights. He's dripping wet and wearing nothing but a too-big bathing suit that's on backwards. He has *freckles*. Adrian is going to be murdered by someone who stepped right out of his elaborate fantasies about finding the perfect boyfriend right before Adelaide's wedding and wowing all of their family who think he's a sadsack who can't keep a man.

"Um," Adrian finally says.

"You took my coat," the guy says. There's something about the way he says it—he has some sort of accent, but it's not the same as the locals, or even from any region he can put his finger on. It's not unpleasant.

"Um," Adrian says again. "Excuse me, what?"

50

"You took my coat," the guy repeats. Adrian blinks at him.

"Sorry?" he says. The guy sighs. He looks almost annoyed.

"I suppose we are to be wed now," the guy says. "At least you are not ugly."

"Thanks—wait! Hey, just 'cause gay marriage is legal now doesn't mean all gays want to get married!" Adrian says, which is . . . probably not the part of the sentence he should have latched on to.

"Why would you take my coat if you did not wish to marry?" the guy says.

"Why did I—Jesus, can we do names? Can we start with names and then maybe move onto why you're in my house and then get to coats or whatever?" Adrian said. "I'm Adrian. I can't keep calling you Hot Burglar in my mind, so—"

Yeah, maybe he's showing his hand a little there.

"Adrian," the guy repeats slowly. "You may call me Finlay."

"So, that's your name?" Adrian asks, because that's a weird way to put it.

"It is close enough to my name for your human tongue," the guy—Finlay—says. And isn't that weird as hell.

"Okay, so, we're old friends now, Adrian and Finlay," Adrian babbles. "So, you know. You're in my house. You need a coat. You're—dripping salt water on my carpet."

Finlay looks down at the carpet and then back up at Adrian. He sighs.

"You have my coat," he repeats. "You took my coat, which means you win my hand."

"I really didn't take a coat," Adrian says slowly, because a memory is starting to come back to him, a story his grandmother used to tell when he and Adelaide were little. A story about fishermen who would steal the skins of seal women to force them into marriage.

It's a story. A story. It's always been a story.

"It was on the beach and you took it," Finlay says. "I watched you."

Holy shit.

"Oh my god, I thought it was my grandmother's!" Adrian says. "I really didn't—I didn't do it on purpose, I swear, I just had all these clothes laid out—" He remembers clearly now, the soft fur coat that smelled like the sea, lying a little further ways down from the clothes he had unpacked from the trunk and laid out in the sun. He was near the end of his packing at that point and shoved it into a box to be dealt with later. He thought it might be worth something--it was soft and beautiful, if incongruous in the attic of a house in South Carolina.

Finlay narrows his blue-green-grey eyes at Adrian. Adrian really wishes he could look away, but they're beautiful.

"I can get it back to you," Adrian adds. "I really—I'm not trying to like . . . trick you into staying with me. I don't need a . . . a husband." Which is maybe a lie, but if he ends up with a husband, he doesn't want to get one like this.

Finlay watches him for another moment and then sighs and sits on the edge of the sofa.

"Where is it?" he asks.

"It's at my house up north," Adrian says. "I sent it in the mail with my grandmother's things. It got mixed up in the clothes, I swear—I shipped them all up to Boston, where I live."

Finlay nods, mostly to himself.

"You have a boat to take us there?" he asks.

"No, no," Adrian says. He's going to wake up from this weird dream any moment now. "Get with the times, man—or, is that insensitive? How often do you come out of the water? You are a—I mean, maybe you're a crazy person, but—" But those eyes are unearthly.

"I am," Finlay says. Then he adds, hesitantly, "I don't go further than the shore. I like—down the shoreline, where the children play. The lights and colors on the dock."

"The boardwalk," Adrian supplies automatically. "Yeah, yeah, that's cool. Um, we're way past boats. We have these things that can fly through the sky, now. We could be home—my home—in three hours . . ."

He trails off. Because there's no way Adrian is getting a sea creature through airport security. Unless he has some kind of seal-boy identification card. The thought makes a hysterical giggle bubble up in Adrian's throat and he has to fight to keep it down.

"Uh, or we could if this was—okay, nevermind the flying thing, we have these other things that can get from place to place faster than boats and on the ground and—"

Finlay puts a hand on Adrian's wrist and he startles into silence. It's a cool touch, cooler than it should be. Adrian shivers.

"Do you have books?" Finlay asks.

"You read?"

Finlay nods.

"I don't—" Adrian starts to say, then spies his phone on the coffee table. "Uh, I think I have something better. Let's—let's get ready to go and I'll show you how to use it."

"Okay," Finlay says, and releases Adrian's wrist.

Oddly, Adrian feels even colder without the touch.

Adrian sets Finlay up with some dry clothes and towels and then retreats to the shower to panic in peace.

Okay. Okay. A mythological being is in his grandmother's bedroom. A sea creature that he's only heard about in stories is, in fact, real and is, in fact, here. And he's gorgeous and that's really just . . . not fair.

Finlay wants his coat back. He *needs* his coat back, if the stories Adrian knows are correct. Without it, he'll spend a lifetime yearning for the sea and forced into a marriage that turns Adrian's stomach. Because . . . well, he's not opposed to getting married, really, or to marrying someone as beautiful as Finlay, but the idea of coercing someone into being with him—it makes him a little sick.

This is a project. This is a task with a beginning, middle, and end, and Adrian is good at those. He's good at organizing, at getting things done, at being ruthlessly efficient. He'll focus on the task at hand and he can freak out over the insanity, the *impossibility* of it later.

He gets out of the shower with a solid plan of action, dresses and packs his suitcases, and heads downstairs where Finlay is already bent over Adrian's phone.

"I figured out how to use your device," he says without looking up.

"Cool," Adrian says, like this is normal. "So, here's the plan--we're gonna pack up the car, swing by the rental place to change my rental agreement, and start heading up north. It's about a fifteen—,sixteen-hour drive, but I can only do about six hours at a stretch before I go crazy, so we'll stop in Virginia for the night and then maybe stop again in New York or Connecticut and then we'll be home and you can have your coat back and like . . . swim off, if you want. Or I could drive you back."

Why did he offer that? Jesus Christ, why did he offer to spend another three days driving? Finlay isn't *that* cute.

"As long as it ends with my coat, I'll be satisfied," Finlay says. He looks up then, pinning Adrian with those cool, depthless eyes.

"Great!" Adrian definitely doesn't squeak. "That's . . . great. Let's . . . let's go."

It's a short drive out of town, but it feels endless. Finlay sits silently in the passenger seat, reading Adrian's iPad, on some sort of Wikipedia spiral and probably using up all of Adrian's monthly data. Jesus, what a conversation that would be with his phone company. *I'm sorry I went over my limit, but I had to reunite a selkie with his coat and he was* super *behind on pop culture and culture in general.*

The car is too quiet. Adrian hasn't even turned on the radio.

"So," he says once they're on the highway. "I've heard the stories but let's just . . . let's go over the basics, okay?"

Finlay looks up from the iPad and blinks at him.

"That would be acceptable," Finlay says.

"Okay," Adrian says. He drums his fingers on the steering wheel. "Okay. Cool. Um, so, you're a selkie."

"Correct," Finlay says.

"So you're like . . . a seal a lot of the time."

"Correct."

"And you can take off your coat and walk as a human."

"Correct."

"And if someone takes your coat, they can force you to marry them?"

"Correct."

Adrian whistles quietly. "God, that sucks," he says. "You have no say in it?"

"Generally we don't," Finlay says. "But we have been raised to protect ourselves. There are . . . ways to encourage a break. It's not always successful. The coat is a powerful tool of persuasion, both on behalf of the selkie and the human who possesses it. They don't mean to hurt us, at least some of the time. And then, of course, there are those selkies that choose to stay."

That's a part of the story Adrian had never heard before.

"Choose?" he asks.

"We observe from the sea, from the edges of humanity," Finlay says. "Occasionally, we see someone worth staying with. Occasionally, we give our coat to those we wish to be with. In those cases, we are able to come and go as we please if we're wronged."

"Huh," Adrian says. "Still . . . the whole stealing a coat thing . . . I mean, in case it's not like, super obvious . . . taking your coat was an accident. I would never force someone to marry me or . . . do anything against their will like that. I don't want you to think I'm like that."

"I don't," Finlay says. He looks at Adrian for a moment, then back down at the iPad. "You seem . . . kind. And I appreciate that."

What the hell can he say to that?

"Well . . . good," Adrian says, and tries to ignore the way his face burns with a flush for the next twenty miles.

The more Finlay reads on the iPad, the more questions he has. Some of them are easy to answer—

"It's like, a dark room with a lot of seats and they just project the pictures real big like on the wall? So everyone can watch the story play out together."

"Interesting."

—and some are harder to answer—

"But how does the craft get up off of the earth and into the sky?"

" . . . uh, science?"

—but he always seems satisfied by whatever it is Adrian is able to tell him. And, interestingly, the more he reads, the more casual his speech and demeanor become. The stiff, formal grammar starts to relax. He starts to use *slang*. It's *weird*.

"Do you eat?" Adrian asks after about four hours on the road.

"Everything eats, Adrian," Finlay says. He actually rolls his eyes. It shouldn't be charming, and yet . . .

"Ha ha," Adrian says. "*What* do you eat?"

"I don't know," Finlay says. "I've never eaten in this form before." He gestures at his body. "Whatever you eat, probably. It's hard to tell what this body wants when I hardly know what's available to it. Well. Mostly hard to tell."

That can't mean what Adrian thinks it means, so he ignores it.

"Pizza!" he says instead. "Let's see if your body likes pizza, okay?"

"Sounds good," Finlay says and he smiles at Adrian, a real, warm smile that makes something twist in the pit of his stomach.

"Good!" Adrian says quickly. "Great, awesome. Super. Let's . . . let's do that."

They pull off the highway and into another tiny beach town, following the winding road until Adrian spies a pizza parlor with spots in its parking lot. He settles Finlay into a booth and then orders them a pizza and a couple bottles of water. When he returns to the booth, Finlay is already looking at him curiously.

"I've told you about me," he says. "About my people. Tell me about you."

"Me?" Adrian says. "Or like, humans? Because I can tell you some stuff about humans and, you know, I know you have the iPad so you can probably look up even more—" He doesn't know why he's panicking, why the idea of telling Finlay about his life is making him nervous. "—there are a lot of people in the world smarter than me, something that probably isn't a surprise after spending a day with me, but—"

Finlay reaches across the table and touches Adrian's hand. Adrian freezes, and not just because Finlay's touch is still a little cooler than he would expect.

"About you," Finlay says. "About Adrian."

"Oh," Adrian says. "Uh. Okay. Great."

He taps his fingers on the table and looks anywhere but at Finlay's face.

"So," he says finally. "Um, there's not much to tell, I guess? I grew up in the area we're headed back to—Boston, up in Massachusetts? My mom and dad split when I was thirteen and we primarily lived with my mom because Dad ended up taking a job in California which is like . . . way all the way at the other end of the country. Like, three thousand miles. So it was me and Mom and my twin sister Adelaide. Uh, pretty normal life. Went to college. Got an art degree. Ended up with an office job that led to another office job, none of which has anything to do with art, but I'm pretty good at it, you know? And that's basically it—I work and I see my mom every couple weeks and I play with my cat and I hang out with some friends . . . just . . . normal. Boring."

"Art?" Finlay asks. "Like, painting?"

"Sort of?" Adrian says. "Um, I draw and I paint a little. I was . . . not bad, really? But you have to be better than 'not bad' to make enough money to live."

"Huh," Finlay says. "I had gotten the impression that art is important to your people."

"Important, yes," Adrian says. "Valued? That's . . . another story."

"That's too bad," Finlay says. "I imagine working with art would make you happy."

Adrian tries to say about three different things in response to that. He settles on, "It would. But I wouldn't say I'm unhappy."

"Are you happy, though?"

"I—" What the *fuck*? "That's a weird question."

"It's an honest question," Finlay says.

Adrian is saved from responding by the arrival of their pizza. The waitress puts it down on the table along with two plates and then *winks* at Adrian, like this is some sort of *date* or something. Adrian tries to ignore her and focus on Finlay, who's looking dubiously at the pizza.

"I Googled this," he says, once the waitress has left.

"And?" Adrian asks.

"I'm not sure I understand it, still."

"It's easy," Adrian says. He reaches over and tugs a piece out of the pie, then holds it up in example. Skeptically, Finlay does the same. Adrian folds the crust just enough to get a good grip and then takes a bite. Finlay does as well. He continues to frown, and then very abruptly his eyes go wide. He chews quickly, then takes another bite, then another.

"Careful!" Adrian says, biting back a laugh. "I wouldn't want you to choke. Small bites—Finlay."

He definitely almost called Finlay "sweetheart," and not with the sassy sarcasm he uses when he calls his friends by the nickname. What the fuck is going on with him? Jesus, it's been too long since he's gotten laid if just sitting in the vicinity of a cute guy is frying his brain this much.

A cute guy who's relying on him entirely. A cute guy who *needs* him. Shit.

They polish off the pizza quickly, even with Adrian urging Finlay to slow down. Adrian pays at the counter and they head back to the car.

"Thank you for buying lunch," Finlay says.

"Hey, it's not like you have any money," Adrian says. "It's not a problem. Really."

"I still appreciate the thought," Finlay says. "Not all humans are as kind as you."

"Don't I fucking know it," Adrian mutters, mostly to himself. To Finlay he says, "Back in the car. Let's do another three hours and then find somewhere I can sleep for a few hours before we go onwards, okay?"

"Okay," Finlay says, but he spends more time looking at Adrian than the iPad as they head back to the interstate.

Adrian does his best to keep the conversation away from the personal as they continue to creep up the east coast. He fills the silence with random facts about anything that pops into his mind and finally resorts to plugging in his phone to turn on some music. Finlay is fascinated by nearly every song and asks a barrage of questions that Adrian answers to the best of his ability. It gets them through the next three hours, through traffic, and off the interstate again as twilight starts to settle.

"Let's get dinner and find a hotel for the night," Adrian says. "Do you sleep? I mean, I guess you do, if you eat, right?"

"I imagine I do," Finlay says. "I haven't tried it yet."

"Are you tired?" Adrian asks.

Finlay pauses to consider this.

"I am," he says. "It's been a long day. There's been a lot to learn. A lot to feel."

"Tell me about it," Adrian mutters. "Chinese take-out and hotel television. Jesus, I'm showing you the dregs of human society. I'm surprised you haven't run screaming back into the ocean already."

"You're doing a wonderful job," Finlay says. "You're fascinating."

It's best for his sanity if Adrian pretends that Finlay is talking about humans on the whole.

"Good to hear," he says faintly. "Let's . . . find somewhere to sleep for the night."

It's a known fact that Chinese restaurants with vague signs in block red letters are universally amazing, so he pulls into the Holiday Inn next to CHINA CAFE and manages to sweet talk them into a discounted rate. He takes a suitcase and tugs Finlay away from the sights and sounds of the lobby and towards the elevator. Finlay stumbles and grabs Adrian's hand to right himself, then doesn't let go. The woman at the desk winks at Adrian as they go by because this is apparently just Adrian's life now.

Or at least for the next two days. Then Finlay will have his coat and be off and Adrian can go back to his regular boring life.

Two days. That's all.

The thought sobers him. Good. He leaves Finlay in the room with the television remote and the Wi-Fi password, then slips out to run across the street and pick up some dinner for them. He could call it in and wait for it to be ready but he really needs some distance, some time to himself. He really needs to think.

It makes sense that he would be attracted to Finlay. Finlay is attractive. He's gorgeous. He's gorgeous and kind of weird in a way that Adrian likes and he's entirely dependent on Adrian and that holds its own appeal. Adrian's just been stockholmed into liking him, has been stuck in a tiny space with him, has been single and lonely for way too long. There's a weird confluence of personal issues and situational issues that's making his body light up in Finlay's presence. It's not emotional, it's not *real*. He'll be a little sad to say goodbye to Finlay, but he will. He'll give him his coat and get rid of him and go back to his stupid boring life and not think about him again.

It takes nearly twenty minutes for Adrian to cross to the restaurant, order, get their food, and walk back. He can't say his head is clear when he returns, but he feels like he's got at least a slightly better handle on the situation.

And then he opens the door and Finlay is sprawled across the bed in a pair of Adrian's boxers and the world is just . . . *cruel*. Jesus, shouldn't selkies be lumpy and round like seals? They definitely shouldn't have six packs. They definitely shouldn't have perfect, warm, brown skin scattered with freckles. They definitely shouldn't look . . . sultry.

"Um," Adrian says. He clears his throat. Finlay blinks at him slowly with sleepy eyes.

"I couldn't figure out how to make the room cooler," he says. Adrian swallows.

"Cool. Yeah. I can. Do that. I brought food?" He holds the bag up and Finlay looks a little more awake. He's watching cartoons, something colorful with songs, something Adrian's never seen before.

"I'm definitely hungry," Finlay says. "More pizza?"

Adrian has to fight a smile despite the panic still enveloping him.

"No, but something equally good," he says. "Or at least, equally easy. Let me turn up the air." He turns towards the thermostat and says, as casually as he can manage, "You might want to put a shirt on. You know. So you don't get too cold."

Adrian divides the food onto the provided paper plates and before long they consume it all as they watch cartoons on separate beds. Finlay laughs at all the jokes, even though it's impossible he has the context for all of them. He has a great laugh.

Adrian forces himself to take a cold shower as he gets ready for bed and sets his alarm for early. If they can get on the road early enough, maybe they can get back to Boston tomorrow and he won't have to deal with another night of this.

"We'll get up early, get breakfast, get on the road," Adrian says. "But I'm exhausted. I need to . . . you know, sleep."

"Right," Finlay says.

Adrian gets under the covers and Finlay follows suit, watching him closely over the space between their beds.

"Adrian," Finlay says, just as Adrian is about to close his eyes and try to convince himself to sleep.

"Yeah?" he asks. He forces a smile.

"You said before your parents 'split,'" Finlay says. "I inferred that meant they were no longer together?"

Okay. There's nothing like his parents' divorce to kill a boner.

"Yeah," Adrian says again. He sighs. "Um, they got married and had me and Addie and . . . I don't know, as time went on, they just felt like they didn't have anything in common anymore? They fought a lot, they didn't really seem to like each other? So they got a divorce."

"They fell out of love," Finlay says.

"If they were ever in love to begin with," Adrian says before he can stop himself.

"Hm," Finlay says.

Adrian sighs again and covers his eyes with his hands. God, this is the fucking last thing he needs to think about on top of the angst of being in tight quarters with a sweet and handsome man.

"It was sort of a marriage of convenience, I think?" Adrian says. "They were bored and alone and attracted to each other and figured 'what the hell?' Which is just . . . stupid. It's a stupid reason to get married. It's a stupid reason to be with someone. You need to feel it. You need to have that connection, you know? And without it, you're just fooling yourself. And to add kids to the mix . . . I don't know. I love my parents, but their marriage was a trainwreck that shouldn't even have lasted as long as it did."

Finlay is quiet across from him.

"You're not married." It's a statement, not a question.

"I'm not," Adrian confirms.

"Hm," Finlay says again.

He doesn't say anything else for a long time, long enough that Adrian eventually falls into a troubled sleep.

Adrian wakes up exhausted and foggy. He slept poorly, plagued by terrible dreams he can't quite remember. His mood must be obvious, because Finlay gives him a wide berth and doesn't press with more questions. He sits quietly in the passenger seat, eating McDonald's hashbrowns with zeal and reading along on the iPad as they head up the coast. He has grand plans of getting them up 95 and into Massachusetts in record time, but every single state has other plans. He hits traffic jam after traffic jam, accident after accident. They've slowed to a crawl, really, covering barely any ground. He tries not to let his irritation slip through, but Finlay lays a hand on his shoulder at the Virginia/Maryland border.

"Do you need to rest?" he asks. "You seem tense."

"I'm fine," Adrian lies. "I'm just . . . tired. I didn't sleep well."

"I'm sorry," Finlay says. He squeezes Adrian's shoulder and he hates himself for the way he relaxes into the touch. He doesn't know Finlay. He shouldn't find comfort in him. He's just a warm body. Warmer, now, that he was when they first met, which is strange, but what about this makes any sense?

"Will your sister be in Massachusetts when we arrive?" Finlay asks after another few miles of passing time with nothing but the music on Adrian's phone.

"My sister?" Adrian asks.

"You said you had a twin sister," Finlay says. "Will I be able to meet her when we get to your home?"

Adrian feels a little sick. Of course Finlay wants to meet Addie. Holy shit, how stupid could Adrian be? Of course the stupid selkie who stumbled into his gran's backyard couldn't be *gay*, what were the odds of *that*?

"She's overseas with her fiancé," Adrian says with perhaps a little more of an edge than he intended.

"Oh," Finlay says. He sounds vaguely disappointed, but not actually upset. Adrian has to stop jumping to conclusions, has to stop stressing himself out. Finlay isn't interested in *anyone*, he's interested in getting his fucking coat back and getting the hell back to the ocean. "She's getting married, then?"

"Yeah," Adrian says. They're not going anywhere. He takes his hands from the wheel and runs them through his hair. "To this guy she met in school. Grad school—that is, school that you go to after college to become better trained in certain fields, I guess? Addie and Franklin's field is business."

"They met at school and fell in love?" Finlay asks. Adrian, begrudgingly, has to nod.

"They did." He may not like Franklin, but he can't deny the guy is crazy about his sister, and he's never seen Adelaide so happy.

"You seem reluctant to talk about it," Finlay says. When Adrian takes to Wikipedia to rewrite the entries on selkies once this is all over, he'll be sure to mention how annoyingly observant they are.

"I don't like her fiancé very much," he admits. "I'm happy she's happy, but he's kind of . . . I don't know. He rubs me the wrong way." He spares a glance to his right. Finlay is gazing at him calmly and attentively. There's a warmth there that's so distracting that he can't look away, doesn't look away until the car behind him leans on its horn and he's startled into lurching forward another twenty feet. He feels himself flush and his favorite defense mechanism kicks in: he starts to babble.

"It's just, Franklin reminds me of this guy I used to date," he says quickly, eyes on the road. "A series of guys, really—I had a type and that type was hot, condescending assholes who thought they were better than me. And Franklin's not really like that, but something about him just reminds me of those guys. Reminds me of—reminds me of Ryan."

He stops before he can dig himself further, but he can already tell it's too late.

"Ryan?" Finlay asks. Adrian sighs.

"This . . . guy," he says slowly. "This guy I dated. Um, proposed to. This guy who didn't want to marry me."

The last thing Adrian wants to do is look at Finlay, but he can't help himself. Then he has to do a double-take because he almost doesn't recognize him. Finlay's posture has gone rigid. His gaze is dark, his lips are curled into a frightening scowl. He looks . . . dangerous.

"Why would he not want to marry *you*?" Finlay manages to say through his obvious anger. Adrian thinks he'll be oddly touched by the gesture if he ever works through his shock.

"Lots of reasons," he says. "Primarily because he didn't love me. Never had, I guess. He thought he could do better. He was just 'passing time.'" He'll never forget the look on Ryan's face when he said that. "He thought I understood he wasn't serious about me."

I mean, you're nice enough, but come on, he had said, but that one still hurts too much to repeat out loud.

"He's a fool," Finlay says. When Adrian looks back to him, he still looks angry, but there's a sadness to it now as well. "He's an . . . an idiot. He made a mistake."

"Yeah, I tend to think I'm the one who made a mistake. A two-year long mistake."

Finlay shakes his head.

"He walked away from you," he says. "He had a chance to be with you and he threw it away. It's his mistake."

Finlay says it with such conviction that Adrian almost believes it. And the way he's staring at Adrian as he says it . . .

"It's in the past," he manages to say.

"Good," Finlay says. He looks back to the road. If Adrian didn't know better, he'd think Finlay was blushing underneath his freckles. "You deserve happiness."

"Thanks," Adrian says quietly.

Neither of them speaks for a long time after that.

Traffic thwarts Adrian's plan to get back to Boston before he's too cross-eyed to drive any longer, so they pull off the highway again somewhere in New York. Adrian's off-kilter enough that he gives in to Finlay's suggestion of pizza for dinner and manages to Yelp a decently reviewed pizza place in East Bumblefuck or wherever they've ended up. At least, he thinks it's decent until they pull up and he sees that it's a pizza place attached to a minigolf course.

Not a lot of options in East Bumblefuck, apparently.

"What's that?" Finlay asks, gesturing towards the course as they exit the car.

"It's like . . . a game?" Adrian says. "It is a game. It's . . . you hit little balls with sticks and try to get them to go into holes and you score points and it's silly but . . . fun."

Finlay nods slowly and then turns to Adrian with pleading, hopeful eyes. He doesn't even say anything. Adrian groans.

"Where did you learn sad puppy eyes, anyway?" he grouses.

"Cartoons," Finlay says. His pout deepens to the point where it's nearly comical. Adrian has to bite back a laugh.

"Fine, fine," he says. "We'll eat and if it's still open when we're done we'll play minigolf."

Finlay's grin lights up his face and makes something flutter in Adrian's chest.

"Thank you!" he says, and Adrian has to look away before he says or does something stupid and impulsive.

The pizza is surprisingly good. The garlic knots are better than good. And, of course, they finish eating with plenty of time to play a round of minigolf.

"We go all night long!" the waitress says. "'Til almost midnight. It's fun for kids, but it's a great date spot, too." And, in the continuing farce that Adrian's life has become, she grins at him slyly and raises her eyebrows on the word "date." Adrian sighs and doesn't bother to correct her.

Finlay, of course, picks up on it. The moment she leaves to run Adrian's credit card and grab them balls and putters, Finlay rounds his gaze squarely on Adrian.

"'Date spot?'" he asks.

"Like . . . courting, I guess?" Adrian says. "Or . . . whatever word you have for the stuff people do before they get married. Like, romantic stuff." He adds quickly, "But a lot of it is stuff you'd do with friends, too. Like, I used to minigolf with my friends all the time, it's just a fun thing to do."

Finlay nods.

"She thinks we're on a date," he says.

"She does," Adrian says carefully, but Finlay just nods and doesn't ask for further clarification.

When they have their putters and balls, Adrian leads Finlay out to the start of the course.

"So," he says, "the point is to get the ball into the hole in as few hits as possible. The stuff around the hole—" He gestures to the legs of the fiberglass elephant standing in the middle of the green. "—is there to throw you off, to get in the way so you have to take more shots. Does that make sense?"

Finlay nods, frowning in concentration.

"Look," Adrian continues. "Watch how those kids up ahead do it."

They turn their gazes to the family two holes ahead of them and watch as both of the children take their turns. Once they're running to the end of the hole to collect their balls from the alligator's mouth, Finlay nods and looks back to their elephant with a resolute expression.

"I'll go first," Adrian says. "Then you can just like . . . copy me."

It's a noble gesture and a good idea, but it would be a better idea if Adrian wasn't garbage at minigolf. His ball bounces off one of the elephant's legs and rolls all the way back to the start.

"Given the rules you explained, I take it I *shouldn't* copy that?" Finlay says, smirking.

"Who taught you sarcasm, anyway?" Adrian mutters, and steps back so Finlay can set up his own shot.

"The internet," he says. He puts his ball down at the starting point and frowns, standing next to it and adjusting his stance and his grip on the putter.

"You should—" Adrian starts to say, but then realizes it would probably be easier just to show him. He steps closer and places a hand on Finlay's hip and immediately remembers why this is a terrible idea. "Um."

Finlay turns to him curiously. Their faces are far too close for Adrian's comfort.

"Yes?"

"Just . . . like this," Adrian says, looking at the ground. He nudges Finlay's hips and feet into a better stance, shifts his hands on the putter. Finlay's skin is warm, now, nearly the same temperature as Adrian's own. He steps back, his hands burning with the contact, and tries to act normal. "Hit it gently."

He does. The ball rolls neatly under the elephant and stops just beside the hole.

"Jesus fuck," Adrian mutters. Finlay smirks again. Finlay might be kind of an asshole.

Adrian really shouldn't like that so much.

Those first shots are an accurate predictor of the rest of the game. Finlay scores ones and twos and threes. Adrian gets a lot of pity sixes.

"You're too aggressive," Finlay says, as if he's the one who's been playing minigolf since he was a kid and Adrian is the one who just stumbled out of the ocean forty-eight hours ago.

"I think no one ever in my life would tell you I was too aggressive," Adrian says. "The opposite, probably. I'm a pushover."

"You let other people have their way," Finlay translates. Adrian has about a million questions about selkie brains. Finlay is picking up on slang at lightning speed. It's a little creepy.

"I do," Adrian says. "It's a pretty ingrained part of my personality at this point. I don't think I could take what I wanted if I tried."

"Your wants and needs are important," Finlay says, raising his eyebrows.

"Yeah, I guess," Adrian says. "Let's . . . let's go on to hole ten, okay?"

Finlay shrugs and leads the way over to the pirate ship towering over hole ten. "What's that supposed to be?" he asks.

It's a distraction. It's an intentional distraction he's throwing to Adrian to change the subject. It makes Adrian a little weak in the knees.

Despite his poor showing and the unexpected veer into Adrian's personal failings, he has a great time playing. It should be stupid or boring, but Finlay is gleeful and just competitive enough to be charmingly smug. He asks a million questions about the animals and objects decorating each hole and Adrian delights in explaining them all to him, if only because he smiles and laughs brightly enough to light up the entire course when he's pleased by the responses. It's fun—it's the most fun that Adrian has had in a while. He can almost forget that he's teaching a seal-boy how to play human games. He can almost pretend he's on a real date.

Finlay scores well enough to win a free return visit and Adrian scores poorly enough that the sardonic teenage attendant gives him a literal "You tried!" sticker, which makes Finlay positively *cackle*.

"I've seen that!" he laughs. "On the internet!"

"Of course you have," Adrian mutters good-naturedly.

"We should come back tomorrow before we leave," Finlay says. "Maybe I can teach you a few things."

"You're not funny," Adrian lies. "Let's go find a hotel so I can sleep off my humiliation."

"It will still be there in the morning, I assure you," Finlay says, and this time Adrian can't hold back his laughter.

A little Googling in the car finds them a nearby hotel that's way classier than Adrian would normally be able to afford anywhere but the middle of nowhere. They check in and go up to their room, still buzzing pleasantly from their game. Finlay peers out the window and taps on it to get Adrian's attention.

"Can we go swimming down there?"

Adrian crosses to the window and looks down. There's a pool just below them, lit up in the dark of the night, with two people swimming laps despite the late hour.

"Uh, I have to check," Adrian says. "Is that . . . okay for you? It's not like the ocean—it's full of like, chemicals and things to keep it clean."

"In this body, as long as it's okay for you, it's okay for me," Finlay says. Adrian still hesitates. Will the pool make him long for the ocean? Will it make him sad? "I'm not tired enough to sleep," Finlay adds. "And I'd like to get wet again."

"Let me check how late it's open," Adrian says, and the smile Finlay gives him in response is worth it.

The pool is open until midnight, and by the time they change into bathing suits (Finlay drops trou in the middle of the room without pause and Adrian nearly has a heart attack in his haste to whirl around), the two people swimming laps are on their way out. They have the whole pool area—the pool and the deck and a fire pit and lounge chairs—to themselves.

Finlay slides into the water like—there's no other way to describe it—a seal. The water barely ripples, barely makes a sound. Even when he surfaces on the other end, grinning from ear to ear, the water remains mostly still. Adrian isn't nearly as graceful. He splashes all over the place slipping into the pool and splashes even more as he swims over to the shallow end while Finlay swims lap after lap. Eventually, he slows to a stop around where the water is about six feet deep. His head pops up from the surface—his eyes look almost clear blue in the light of the fire pit—and when it's clear he's going to tread water for a bit, Adrian swims over to him.

"How is it?" he asks.

"Not quite like home," Finlay says. "But lovely all the same."

"Do you miss the ocean?" Adrian asks before he can stop himself.

Finlay frowns thoughtfully and brushes his wet hair off of his forehead.

"I miss swimming," he finally says. "I miss the comfort of the familiar. I don't know that I miss the ocean in particular. At least, not yet. I'm still absorbing the world around me. There's more to the human world than I imagined. I think I understand why people choose to stay."

In the low light, Adrian would swear Finlay's eyes change color again, from ice blue to dark brown and then back to their usually stormy color. He smiles softly, almost self-deprecatingly. All Adrian can do is nod.

"Do you have a family? People waiting for you?" he asks.

"Not any longer," Finlay says. "My parents are long gone. My sisters are paired off."

"No, like . . . partner seal?" Adrian asks. He hopes the low light hides his flush. He can't fucking believe he just asked that.

"No," Finlay says, smiling again. Adrian falters in his water tread and almost sinks below the surface. Finlay grabs his arm and pulls him back up until he's stable. "And you? Your sister is away, your father is elsewhere . . . do you have family missing you? A partner human?"

"Oh, shut up, you know what I meant," Adrian says. "And no. I don't know, I got fucked up after Ryan dumped me. Fucked up about relationships, I mean. I've dated a couple guys since, but mostly . . . there's no spark, I guess. And I'm getting older, in human years, at least. I don't want to date a bunch of guys I'm not super into just for the sake of it. I want to be with someone who cares about me. I want to be with someone I care about."

Finlay nods, his eyes serious, and Adrian doesn't add that he thought he was broken, that he'd never feel that spark again, that he'd never care about anyone again. And then some stupid seal-boy showed up in his grandmother's living room. If nothing else, he owes Finlay for showing him that his heart wasn't completely crushed by Ryan's rejection.

"I understand," he says. "And I'm sorry, again. About the man who left you. I still can't fathom it."

"There's not much to fathom," Adrian says. "I'm quiet and boring and spend too much time making budgets and drawing and playing with my cat. I'm not exactly a catch."

"You're wrong," Finlay says. He stares at Adrian and Adrian stares back, his heart in his throat. Then, expression dead serious, eyes grave, Finlay reaches over and—

Dunks Adrian under the water.

Adrian pushes himself to the surface and breaks above it, sputtering.

"You asshole!" he says. Finlay laughs, high and clear, and takes off across the pool.

Adrian chases after him, and that's how they spend the next hour. Finlay lets Adrian win a handful of times—he must, there's no way Adrian can out swim a *selkie*—and they climb out, exhausted and laughing, once Adrian's arms feel too rubbery to go on.

"I'll sleep well, at least," he says as they dry off. "Jesus, I can't remember the last time I've been this exhausted."

"Are you feeling better, though?" Finlay asks. He pulls open the door to the hotel and then shivers violently as the air conditioning hits them.

Adrian wraps an arm around him without even thinking about it, pulling Finlay against him, into the cocoon of his towel.

"Feeling better?" Adrian asks, and is pleased that his voice isn't as high and panicked as he thought it might be once the reality of Finlay's skin against his own dawned on him.

"You were . . . you were . . ." Finlay frowns. "Sad," he settles on. "You were sad this morning."

He was, a bit. Selkies are too damned perceptive.

"I am," Adrian says. "Feeling better, I mean. Thanks."

"I'm happy to help," Finlay says. "I like it when you're happy."

Adrian bites his bottom lip and tries out a few responses in his head. He settles with, "Same, really," and Finlay bestows another beaming smile on him.

Back up in the room, they change for bed, Adrian retreating into the bathroom before Finlay can strip in front of him again. When he emerges, Finlay's already in his borrowed pajamas and wrapped in a hotel robe. He's still shivering.

"I can turn down the air conditioning," Adrian says, already moving to the thermostat. "Your teeth are practically chattering."

"Body temperature adjustment," Finlay explains. "It's a slow process when we take this form, moving from the sea to the air. And the artificial environments human establish—it's difficult to regulate."

"I'll bet," Adrian says. He raises the temperature into the low seventies, his own preference for arctic level a/c be damned. Finlay is huddled on the edge of one of the beds, and Adrian sits next to him, wrapping an arm around him and rubbing his arm vigorously. "Jesus, I don't know why you guys bother coming up here at all."

"The world above has a lot to offer," Finlay says. "It's a risk, of course. It's always a risk that someone will find your coat and you'll be trapped. But it's a much more vibrant world than the one beneath the waves, in many ways. There are many things that make it worth the risk."

"I can't believe that people would do that to you," Adrian murmurs. "I can't believe that's something you need to worry about. I can't believe humans can be that heartless."

Adrian's slowed the movement of his hand to a gentle stroke from shoulder to wrist. He's starting to feel the heat of Finlay's body through the robe. Finlay's teeth aren't chattering any longer. He's not shivering.

He's looking at Adrian, actually, just looking. He has beautiful, long eyelashes that Adrian never noticed before, and they flutter over the freckles on his cheekbones when he blinks his eyes.

"Adrian," he says quietly.

And Adrian doesn't know what comes over him, what seizes him in that moment. It's more than lust—he knows from lust, he knows how to control it. It's something else, something new and small and soft between them, something that Adrian has been aching for.

He reaches out and curls his hand around the edge of Finlay's jaw and kisses him.

Finlay's mouth is warm and gentle against his. He should taste like pizza and ginger ale and the M&Ms they ate in the car on the drive to the hotel, but Adrian can still, incongruously, taste the sea on his lips. He smells like the sea, too, not the chlorine of the pool, and it's oddly comforting. The feel of Finlay's hands on his shoulders is comforting, *Finlay* is comforting, sitting so close Adrian can feel his body heat, a steadying presence, the calm in the middle of the chaos of the last few days. Finlay is the cause of the chaos, so he shouldn't be the solution too, but Adrian can't argue with results.

He pulls away to take a breath and abruptly realizes what he's done.

"Oh holy shit," Adrian whispers. He stumbles haltingly to his feet. "Oh, *shit*, Finlay, I'm sorry."

"Adrian—"

"I shouldn't have—here I am telling you I'm not like those people, that I wouldn't—and I did! I shouldn't have—"

"Adrian!" Finlay says again and gets to his feet, taking a step forward.

"No, no, no," Adrian says. He can't catch his breath. "Oh my god, I'm—I'm just so sorry."

He backs into the door and opens it, grabbing his hoodie with the hotel key card nestled next to the rental car keys. He trips out into the hallway and slams the door behind him.

In the hallway, he can breathe again, but the pounding in his brain telling him just how badly he fucked up is even louder without the blood rushing past his ears to quiet it. He walks quickly towards the elevator. He's not sure where he's going, what he's going to do, but he needs to put some distance between himself and Finlay. He needs to give Finlay some space; that's the best way to apologize right now.

He's an idiot. He's worse than an idiot, he threw himself at Finlay, he took advantage of Finlay after all these days of talking about how upsetting he finds that traditional selkie myth. He promised Finlay he wasn't like the people in the stories, that he wouldn't force Finlay to do anything against his will, and then he goes and . . . and *kisses him.*

Inside the elevator, Adrian closes his eyes and sinks his hands into his hair. When he squeezes his fingers together, the pinpricks of pain on his scalp help him shake the fog of shame and confusion, but don't offer much clarity. They still have nearly four hours in the car to get to Boston. He'll be lucky if Finlay dares to finish the journey with him. Maybe he should just buy him a bus ticket and meet him in Boston. Maybe he should just give him the keys and tell him where to go and where to look—it took him ten minutes to figure out how an iPhone works, driving a car can't be that much harder.

The car is where Adrian ends up. There's nowhere else to go. He can't abandon Finlay at the hotel and he doesn't have his wallet, anyway. Hell, he doesn't even have shoes. He does have the car keys, so he curls up in the backseat, alone with his thoughts, with the lingering shame left behind by his actions.

Fuck, fuck, fuck. The worst of it—and god, how embarrassed is he that *this* is what he considers the worst of it—is that even if Finlay did like him, even if Finlay thought that maybe something could happen between them, those chances are dead in the water.

Fuck, fuck, fuck.

Adrian wakes up to a sharp knock on the window. He sits up abruptly and hits his head on the side of the door, already making up excuses for the cop that's sure to be asking him what a scruffy-looking Latino kid is doing sleeping in the back of a new car in the parking lot of a nice hotel. He's surprised, then, to see Finlay standing outside of the window, peering in at him, face blank. He's holding the suitcase they brought up to the room with them. He looks way too good given how shitty Adrian feels.

He slowly opens the door and steps out into the parking lot. Finlay gives him a wide berth. Of course he does.

"I checked out at the desk," he tells Adrian with the same blank expression. Adrian stretches in an attempt to work out the aches that come from sleeping curled up in the back of a sedan. "I wasn't entirely sure what to do, so when she asked if I should just put it on the same card, I said yes." He reaches into his pocket and pulls out Adrian's wallet, handing it over to him. Adrian makes sure their fingers don't brush together when he takes it.

"Okay," he says.

"I brought you coffee," Finlay adds. He gestures towards the car, and Adrian turns around. There's a takeaway cup of coffee and a plate with some continental breakfast-style pastries sitting on the roof of the car. "I know you were desperate for it yesterday."

"Thanks," Adrian says quietly. He can't look Finlay in the eye. Christ. Christ, he fucked up. "I guess we should get going. We have a lot of ground to cover."

"Adrian—" Finlay starts to say, but Adrian grabs the suitcase and turns away, stowing it in the trunk. He takes his time getting it settled with the rest of his crap, finding his shoes, switching out his sleep shirt for a clean t-shirt, pulling jeans over his boxers, and by the time he slams the trunk closed, Finlay is already in the passenger seat. Adrian breathes out, then takes a deep breath. This might be the last time he can breathe easily until Finlay has his coat and is on his way back home.

When he gets back into the car, he can feel Finlay turn to him.

"Adrian—" he starts to say again, but Adrian just starts the engine and plugs in his phone. He turns the music on as loud as he can stand it, focuses on the road in front of him, and begins the last leg of the journey home.

They make it through the rest of New York and Connecticut without speaking. They make it into Massachusetts. They make it onto the turnpike before Finlay opens his mouth again.

"This is where you live?" he asks. Adrian turned the music down about fifty miles ago, when it became clear Finlay got the picture and wasn't going to try and speak to him.

"Ish," Adrian says. He tries to make his voice sound normal. "This is the western part of the state. Where I live, it's a little more suburban. It's by the city."

Finlay hums softly. When Adrian chances a glance in his direction, he's staring out at the scenery as it flies by. He looks beautiful. He looks so beautiful that Adrian feels like an idiot for ever thinking something could happen between them. Sweet, beautiful men don't fall in love with him, let alone sweet, beautiful mythological creatures.

It's early enough in the day that there's not much traffic heading down the pike and towards the city. It feels like no time at all until they're exiting the highway, twisting and turning through the suburban streets, right up to Adrian's front door.

He pulls into the driveway and cuts the engine. They sit in silence.

"Is *this* where you live?" Finlay asks. Adrian nods. "I like it."

He has no idea what to say to that.

"Come on, let's go find your coat," Adrian says in a quiet monotone. Finlay turns to him, but Adrian ignores him and gets out of the car, heading towards the house. There's a note on the front door from his next door neighbor that he tears off as he pulls out his keys with his other hand.

Adri—

Brought your mail in, including the boxes. Fed Tris. Sorry about your gran. Let's do brunch soon—come over when you're back home.

—Preeta

He shoves the note in his pocket. The idea of talking to anyone sounds like a chore right now. What would he say? How could he describe the past few days? *Oh, hey, so selkies are real and I accidentally stole one's coat and, while nobly returning it to him, tried to jump him in a hotel room.*

He pushes open the front door and steps inside. Finlay is on his heels.

The house is nearly just like he left it—books piled haphazardly on the coffee table, a collection of mugs by the sink in the kitchen, sweaters and hoodies draped over the back of chairs. The only signs he was gone are the mail piled neatly on the table by the door and the stacks of boxes lining the wall next to the stairs.

"It's in one of these," Adrian says to Finlay, and kneels down to squint at the labels, trying to remember which boxes he put what inside, trying to sort them by date sent at the very least. Behind him, he hears Finlay's footsteps, tapping across the scuffed wood floors, followed by a creak from the stairs. He glances up at Finlay covertly from under his bangs. He's scaling the stairs, peering at the art Adrian has hanging there, trailing his fingers just in front of the glass. Then he's up another stair and another and out of sight.

Which is good. Adrian needs to focus.

He finally finds the last box. It's on the bottom of one of the stacks, which seems stupid, but he digs it out and tears the tape with his house key. Buried under some old sweaters and the dress his mother wore to her quinceañera is Finlay's coat.

It's as soft as he remembered, the same brown-silver as Finlay's hair and dappled with darker spots that remind him of Finlay's freckles. It still smells of the sea, but refreshingly, not like the musty, salt-scent of the boxes that were stored in his grandmother's attic. He runs his hands over it and remembers, for a moment, the feeling of having his hands in Finlay's hair.

He closes his eyes.

He could hide the coat. He could lock it in a closet, run across the street and ask Preeta to hide it, throw it in the trunk of his car and peel off the office and lock it in the supply cabinet across from his desk. He could keep it. He could keep Finlay.

It's an ugly, awful thought, and he goes hot with embarrassment just knowing that he entertained it, even for a moment.

"Finlay!" he calls up the stairs. His voice wobbles in the middle. He clears his throat. "Finlay! I found your coat!"

There's no response from the second floor—maybe Finlay's found his computer or some book or another that's caught his attention. Adrian sighs and gets to his feet, climbing the stairs to the tiny second floor of his tiny house.

Finlay isn't in the bathroom or the closet-sized office. He's in Adrian's bedroom, petting Tristan, who's curled up on the window seat. With the sunlight filtering in through the curtains and Tristan purring beneath Finlay's fingers, it's almost like Adrian has stumbled into a painting or a photograph.

He clears his throat again and Finlay looks up.

"Is this your cat?" he asks. Then, "I'm sorry, that's stupid, of course he is. He's in your house."

"It's not stupid," Adrian says softly. "His name is Tristan."

Finlay smiles. Adrian hadn't realized how much he missed it. How is it he could become so attached to a smile in only three days?

"Hello, Tristan," he says, and scratches the cat behind the ears. Tristan purrs. Tristan never purrs. Tristan is an asshole—that's why Adrian ended up with him and Adelaide ended up with his sweet-tempered brother and sister when their mother's cat had kittens.

"I have your coat," Adrian says before he can get emotional about seeing this beautiful man be affectionate with his asshole cat. He thrusts the coat out towards Finlay. Finlay looks up warily and approaches Adrian. He curls his fingers around the edge of the coat and it seems to heat up in Adrian's hand. Finlay's eyes flash pure, ice blue, then turn a dark, muddy brown. It's mesmerizing.

Adrian releases the coat.

"I'm sorry," he says again, swallowing hard. "I'm sorry I kissed you. I don't care about the lure of the coat or anything like that. I shouldn't have done it. I should have known better. I like you, Finlay. I respect you. I didn't mean to tarnish either of those things."

Finlay nods and pulls the coat to his chest, hugging it against himself with both arms. His eyes have settled back into the color they were before, blue-green-grey, the color of the ocean. He stares at Adrian, then holds the coat out to Adrian.

"What do you need?" Adrian asks. "Is it the wrong coat?" He knows it's not. Something in him knows that coat is inhuman, the same thing that knew Finlay wasn't exactly human, that didn't question when he realized, absurdly, that he was faced with a mythological creature. He *knew*. He knows now.

"Take the coat," Finlay says.

"I—no, I'm giving it back," Adrian says. "I didn't mean to take it, I told you, you're free."

"Take the coat, Adrian," Finlay says, and steps forward, pressing it against Adrian's chest. Adrian's arms come up automatically, hugging it against himself to keep it from falling to the floor.

"What—" he starts to say, but then Finlay steps forward and kisses him.

Finlay's hands are warm where they're cupping his jaw, pulling him closer. He kisses like he was born to do it, all smooth and practiced, like he knows exactly how to drive Adrian crazy. Or maybe it's just that anything Finlay does will drive him crazy, maybe it's just three days of quiet *wanting* making even the barest of affection feel like sensory overload. Finlay's lips slide against his own. His mouth opens and they part for just a second, sharing a breath, before Finlay captures his lips again and pulls his even closer, licking against the seam of his lips, the front of his teeth, into his mouth. He presses himself against Adrian. Adrian can, impossibly, feel his body heat even through the coat that's trapped between them, along with Adrian's arms.

Finlay releases him and steps back. He's definitely blushing this time, flushed and panting, his hands shaking as he wipes his mouth and pushes his hair back.

"You didn't do anything wrong," he says, taking advantage of Adrian's shocked silence. "I wanted you to kiss me. It wasn't the coat, it wasn't anything magical. I wanted you to do it."

Adrian's mind is still nothing but fireworks and shock and disbelief. He struggles for words, for the questions he wants to ask. The longer he stays quiet, the more concerned Finlay's expression becomes.

"Unless . . . unless it was the coat," Finlay says softly. "If it was—if *you* didn't want to—this is non-binding, you can give it back, you don't have to—"

"No!" Adrian says sharply. He almost trips over himself in his haste to get to Finlay. "No, no, no, I want you, I've wanted you, it's insane, it doesn't make any sense, I'm crazy about you, you shouldn't be able to meet someone and fall in love this quickly but—" His eyes go wide as he realizes what he's said. "I mean, forget that, that's—I didn't mean—"

Finlay grabs the coat from him, tosses it on the window seat, and pulls Adrian snugly against him. Then they're kissing again, warm—no, hot. Hot and slick, teeth and lips and Finlay's hands in his hair, Finlay's body pressed against his, Finlay's breath coming fast, Finlay's heart beating double time under Adrian's hands. Adrian can move his hands this time, can touch Finlay's hair, his throat, the firm muscles of his back, the dip of his waist. He can press himself against Finlay. He can taste the sea in Finlay's mouth, on his skin, on his throat, he can hear the soft, needy sounds that Finlay makes, he can breathe again, breathe easily for the first time since last night, since the moment he realized what he had done and pulled away from Finlay's mouth.

How stupid, how monumentally stupid. As if there's anywhere else worth being. As if there's anywhere else he wants to be, anywhere beyond right here, right now.

"You're staying?" Adrian asks hoarsely when Finlay shoves him back onto the bed and starts to peel his own shirt off. "You can't—you can't do this and then leave, I can't do this and then have you leave—"

"I'm staying," Finlay says. He slows down, sitting on the edge of the bed. He's still shirtless, which is distracting, but equally distracting is the gravity in his eyes. "I wouldn't leave you. I don't understand how anyone could."

Adrian's not going to cry. He's not.

"What about the ocean?" Adrian asks. "Aren't you—in the stories, the selkies yearn for the ocean."

"In the stories, the selkies don't make their own choices," Finlay says. He takes Adrian's hand and squeezes it. "In the stories, the selkies are torn away from home." He pauses for a moment. "In the stories, there aren't planes and cars and trains that can take them to the ocean to visit on weekends."

Adrian bursts out laughing. If some tears trickle out too, well. Who can blame him?

"We'll keep Gran's house," he promises, brushing Finlay's hair behind his ears. "We'll visit whenever you want. Anything you want-- we'll move to the North Shore if you want, though it's cold as balls, so you might change your mind about the ocean. But anything you want."

"Just you," Finlay says.

And it's a terrible line, it's an awful line from an awful rom-com, but Adrian's heart swells in his chest to hear it. He pulls Finlay into another kiss and another and another.

The coat lays forgotten on the window seat for the rest of the night.

Refurbished

Lara Eckener

Rubbing alcohol, spilled out over
Table, stripped bare by
Paint thinner, rusty can of
Moonshine, rocks glass cross hatched
Knife, paring and spare
Magnets, collected in

This starter kit for how to peel
away the things holding us back.

To want forever is to measure out
ourselves against time, to coil
and tunnel and burrow clockwise,
and study the infinite stretch
of space between seconds.
If we could feel things small enough
maybe we could slip through,
live in the cracks, immortal.

To want it all is a different thing
to look out and not in, to bleed
into the world, the galaxy, the
universe stretching infinite in
the space between breaths where
we drink from the wrong container
without noticing because every

one of them burns, which is nothing
compared to the knife in the cracks
of fingerprints on wet shaking hands.

There are religions that offer to
burn away the skin tying us to the
places we've come to resent, thinking
we'll turn ourselves into paper
and kindling, devotion and truth,
as if answers would make us happier
than the knowledge that there's
always one more question at the end
of hope's desperate response.
Happiness comes more quickly when
we can build it into ourselves.
These magnets let us feel a pulse
not many know is there, caress
the shivering heart of the world.

The starter kit for omniscience consists
of knowing there's always more.

Dear Author

Christine Ricketts

*D*ear Author. Thank you for your submission. Unfortunately at this time...

The words continued on, filling a short, neat paragraph in the center of the page. But as he continued to stare down at them, they all blurred together to form a single word displayed in all caps.

REJECTED.

He crumpled the letter into a tight wad and smashed his hands together, squeezing tightly, as if he could force the paper from existence with enough pressure. Just as abruptly he stopped, dropping the ball to his desk and smoothing the paper back out with short, hurried strokes.

He could write them back. He would write them back. He would just write them back and explain. Maybe his first letter hadn't done a good enough job outlining the book. Or maybe he should have sent a different sample, a different section of the story.

He should have sent the entire book. That was it.

How could they judge his book and his story if they weren't able to read the whole thing? He'd send it tomorrow.

Or, better yet, maybe he should hand deliver it.

Yes, he should take it there himself. Then he could talk to the agent, face to face, and then he or she would understand how special it was. How good it was. If they just knew how hard he had worked on it. How long. If they just knew all about him—

—then they'd understand.

He'd have to make another copy. He couldn't very well take the original. If he took the original, the might try and steal it. They'd take it and they'd say, "Oh yes Mr. Felder, we'd love to read your story." And then they'd take it and publish it under someone else's name and he'd get nothing. Nothing. When he tried to protest, they'd be all "Oh, we're so sorry but we've never heard of you before. You must be mistaken," because they're liars and cheats and he'd have no proof because he hadn't been smart and hadn't made a copy. So he'd be smart. And he'd make a copy.

He would write it out tonight, nice and slow, nice and neat, so that every single word was readable. He wouldn't want to mess up a single word because every word was important to the story and if they didn't read the words right, then they wouldn't understand the story and they might not like it.

What if they didn't like his story?

But of course they'd like it. Because he would be right there to explain it to them if they had any questions.

Or, better yet, he would read it to them! That way there would be no chance of them reading the wrong words. He knew all the words by heart.

Except, he didn't like to read out loud in public very often because sometimes people would interrupt and ask stupid questions or say mean things like, "Where is Main Street" or "Are you going to buy that or just look at it" and he *hated* when people interrupted him.

So he'd just have to make sure that no one interrupted him. That would be so easy. He'd just say, "I'm going to read you my story now. Don't anyone interrupt me." If anyone tried to protest, then he'd just stick his gun in their face and that would shut them up because no one talks when you stick a gun in their face.

Then he would read his story and everyone would sit quietly and listen. When he finished they would all tell him how good it was and how much they liked it. Then they would print a million copies and everyone in the world would read it and he would get to go on TV and people would ask him how he wrote such an amazing story and he would tell them about how he read all those other stories about space and dragons and cowboys and pirates and how he just took words from each book and carefully wrote them over and over on a page until they became his. Those stories became his story. And no one would read those stories anymore because they were all in his story and his story was so much better than the others.

No one would ever read another story because if he saw them he'd just kill them. He'd just kill them and then take their story and burn it, burn all the stories—burn everything—

"Hey. Hey, what's going on in there?" There was a sharp rap of wood against metal.

Blinking, he looked up from his bed where he was methodically shredding paper into a pile. On the other side of the cell door stood a guard. He rapped his nightstick against the bars again.

"You keep ripping up your mail and no one will send you any," the guard warned. With that, he walked away, his echoing footsteps on the concrete the only part of his presence that lingered.

With a growing sense of horror, he realized that the pages he was ripping into tiny pieces were the pages of his manuscript that he had laboriously copied by hand. Hours and hours of work, torn into bite-sized pieces. He stared down at the pile and for a moment, felt a bleak, seemingly endless pit of despair open up inside of him. He wanted to put his head back and howl with the agony boiling up inside of him. He opened his mouth wide—

—and then smiled. It was okay. He had the whole story in his head. He didn't need to write it down at all.

He just needed someone to tell it to.

Part III

Love

1. An intense feeling of deep affection.

First Date

Kaitlyn Sudol

Tuesday starts off with a series of mistakes.

Mistake #1: Coffee. Talia drinks coffee about once a month and violently regrets it every time, cursing expressively as she jitters through her day, awake, yes, but at what cost? The point of being her own boss is, in theory, setting her own hours so her night job and her day job don't interfere with each other, but she's not great at boundaries and at least once a month that equates to sucking down a coffee so she doesn't look hung over when she meets a client.

So Tuesday starts on line at Starbucks, shifting from foot to foot, massaging her temples, and wondering what she can possibly order that will taste as little like coffee as possible. When she gets to the counter, she settles on a white chocolate mocha and the cashier says some completely absurd number that gets even more absurd when she realizes that she's wearing the wrong jacket.

Her mistakes, then, are hastily renumbered.

Mistake #1: Not hanging her coat up on the right hook last night.

Mistake #2: Taking her night job coat instead of her day job coat this morning.

Mistake #3: Coffee.

Mistake #4: Ordering coffee with a mile-long line behind her without realizing that she does not have her wallet with her.

"Uh," she says to the cashier, who's raising one condescending, pierced eyebrow as Talia briefly considers bartering her pocket knife and chalk dust for a shot of espresso.

"I've got it," says the girl in line behind her, and Talia turns around.

Mistake #5: Turning around.

Because. The girl is. Wow.

Talia doesn't necessarily have a type; in high school her type was "outrageous enough to piss off her parents," and in college her type was "doesn't ask too many questions," and in the five or six years since her type has been "anyone on OKCupid willing to go on a date with her." So no, she doesn't have a type, per se, but she's pretty sure that the girl in line behind her would be anyone's. She's maybe an inch or two taller than Talia, curvy, with a spray of freckles across her face and her red hair done up in a braid crown. She's wearing a dress the same blue as her eyes, covered in little hearts. Her phone case has a quote from *Parks and Recreation* on the back of it. Next to Talia's greasy bedhead (the perils of short hair) and dark jeans-dark sweater-dark jacket ensemble, she looks like a goddess. Talia might be in love.

"Uh," she says again, and the girl nudges past her to hand the cashier her phone.

"And a grande red eye with room," she says, and the cashier hits a few more buttons, then scans the girl's phone and hands it back to her.

"Name?" the cashier asks, which is good, because Talia doesn't think she has enough higher brain function to ask herself.

"Anna," the girl says, and the cashier writes it sloppily on both cups in sharpie marker before Talia can correct her.

They step away from the line. The girl—Anna—is still smiling, like the whole thing is a little funny to her, like she has plenty of time and good humor to spare to laugh at Starbucks at 7 a.m.

"You didn't have to do that," Talia finally manages to say. "But, uh, thanks."

"No problem," Anna says. "I've been there, and I know I would murder someone without enough caffeine, so best to prevent future crimes, right?"

"You could have abandoned me to, like, barter, though," Talia says, shoving her hands in her jacket pockets, which is just another reminder of mistake number two.

"Maybe I still will," Anna says. Her smile turns a little sly, a little mysterious, and she adds, "What do you have that's worth this coffee?"

"Not much," Talia admits. "A pocket knife, my house keys, some chalk dust, gum, and I think there's a busted iPhone cable in my inner pocket."

"You're right, it's not much worth trading for. I guess you'll just have to sit with me and talk to work off your debt."

And even though she shouldn't, Talia can't just walk away from a pick-up line delivered that smoothly and effortlessly. It would be disrespectful to the art of flirting as a whole.

"What's your name?" Anna asks, and Talia stares at her blankly for a moment as she tries to remember. She hopes this is another thing Anna will blame on the lack of caffeine.

"Talia," she finally manages to say. "My name is Talia. Sorry. It's just—" *You're so cute and my brain is fried and the exorcism I performed last night wasn't half as exhausting as the three hour argument I had with a disgruntled ghost from the 1970s who refused to leave the vintage stand mixer she was haunting.* "—early."

"I feel you," Anna says. At Talia's raised eyebrow, she adds, "This is my second cup. And I've been up for a while. I've already stumbled through the zombie stagger out of bed and into the waking world."

The barista calls Anna's name, then, and they collect their drinks. Talia watches Anna pour a really ungodly amount of sugar and milk into her coffee and then they settle into a corner table in the sun. It makes Anna's hair glow copper. Talia is so smitten she wants to puke.

"Do you work around here?" Anna asks after a moment of awkward silence where Talia stares at the lid of her cup to avoid giving Anna really embarrassingly obvious heart-eyes.

"No," Talia says. "I work from home mostly, actually? I'm a freelance graphic designer. But I'm meeting a client in this part of town a little later."

"Aw, that's too bad," Anna says. "I work up the street and I wouldn't object to, you know, seeing you around town." And if that wasn't an obvious line, the smile she gives Talia after it would seal the deal. She is flirting with Talia within an inch of her life. Talia regrets being the most awkward and complicated human being to ever live.

"I mean," she tries, hoping her smile looks sincere and not like an animal frozen in a spotlight, "I could . . . see you around town . . . again . . . if you . . . wanted?"

If the world were a just place, the ground would swallow her up, but, miraculously, Anna isn't put off.

"We'll see where the morning takes us," Anna says, grinning, and Talia wonders not for the first time since she entered the coffee shop if she didn't wake up in a romantic comedy. She might as well go for it—it can't be worse than the horror movie that her life normally resembles.

She learns that, number one, Anna works for the city managing endowments and grants. Number two, Anna loves her job because she loves numbers and because it's flexible enough that she can volunteer in her off hours. Number three, Anna lives by herself and had a bad break-up with a woman who must clearly be insane, because Anna is perfect.

"She had some issues with my lifestyle," she tells Talia. Talia has some issues with her taste.

For Talia's part, she does her best to make the boring half of her life sound exciting without actually talking about the exciting part of her life. It's not easy—she can say "I have a large collection of succulents" with a big smile all she wants, but it doesn't make it actually sound *interesting*. Sure, people think "graphic designer" sounds glamorous, but that's before she admits it's about 10% designing within very strict specifications and 90% wrangling needy clients.

Needy clients. Shit. Mistake #6.

"Oh crap," she says, rudely interrupting as Anna is describing her dog. "Clients! Shit! I have a client!" They've been talking for over half an hour. She's still ten minutes away and her appointment is supposed to start momentarily.

"Oh no!" Anna says. "I'm so sorry, I didn't mean to keep you—"

"No, no, no," Talia says. "I lost track of time, I don't know why my alarm didn't go off, shit!" She chugs the rest of her coffee, wincing at the aftertaste, and jumps to her feet.

"Still, I shouldn't have kept you and I shouldn't keep you any further, but maybe you want to do this again sometime? Because I think you're cute and *I'd* really like to do this again sometime."

Talia's defenses are down enough that she makes a pathetic, desperate, swoony sound at that. A cute girl thinks she's cute.

"Yes, definitely, I'd love that, I'm sorry I'm the most awkward human being alive." And probably one of the most awkward dead ones. She would know.

"You're not," Anna says, "really." She hands her phone to Talia—the "Contacts" page is open. Talia quickly adds her information and then hits

"Done" and hands the phone back to Anna. "I'll text you later. Go on, before you're even later!"

If Talia were a) more confident, b) less late, or c) more well-rested, she might have hugged, or even kissed, Anna before dashing out. She's none of those things, however, so she gives Anna another deer-in-headlights smile and then dashes out of the Starbucks and up the street, not entirely convinced that the morning so far hasn't been a very nice dream.

Mistakes #7 through about #17 are all variations of "making the terrible decision to freelance to assholes like this, oh god save me" and start with the very rude lecture her 8 a.m. client gives her and end with her 5 p.m. client telling her he could make a poster that's just as nice in Microsoft Word. She doesn't set him on fire with her mind, but not from lack of trying.

The only highlight of the day is the text she gets halfway through her 8 a.m. appointment.

Hi, this is Anna from Starbucks. Are you free to talk later tonight? I'm old-fashioned that way.

There's a winky face emoji at the end. It gives her just enough energy to power through the rest of her day.

When she gets home, she feels Elijah before she sees him, which isn't unusual. He likes to read her before he decides whether or not to materialize; sometimes if she's had a shit day, she doesn't see him until she's pouring a glass of wine. Today, though, he appears in front of her as she angrily sheds her night job jacket and puts it back on the correct hook.

"I'm sorry everyone living is an idiot," he says as he shimmers into existence. "If it makes you feel better, most dead people are idiots too."

"I know that," she mutters. "Present company, for example."

"Oh, so it's one of *those* days."

"Can it, E," she says, and swats completely ineffectually at him. She shivers when her hand passes through his arm and then marches over to the couch, where she collapses in an exhausted lump.

"My poor baby," he says, and settles into the armchair. Or over it. Despite being around ghosts since around the time she hit puberty, she's still not entirely clear on how incorporeal beings interact with solid objects. She doesn't think most incorporeal beings are clear on it either. Elijah isn't, at least, despite being a ghost for over two-and-a-quarter centuries.

"Today was a series of mistakes." She opens her eyes and rolls onto her side to stare balefully up at him. He's sympathetic, at least, which she appreciates. As she once pointed out to him, Talia is Elijah's best friend because the number of people able to see and interact with him is minimal; in other words, he has no other choice. Elijah is Talia's best friend because human interaction is exhausting, explaining her night job is exhausting, and it's just easier to rely on someone who has no other choice but to befriend her.

Talia sort of inherited Elijah from her aunt. When she was in sixth grade and started hearing voices that weren't there, it only took her mother a few weeks to figure out what was going on. After a very awkward conversation with Talia's father about things like the existence of a spirit world, the places that world overlaps with our own, and the sensitivity to it that's been in her family for several generations, she dropped Talia off with her Aunt Rosa.

Rosa was a psychic; she read tarot cards for $3.99 a minute over the phone and the palms of anyone who was pulled in by the neon sign hanging in the front window of her parlor. She turned off the sign once Talia was settled on the couch with a soda, shrugged off the mound of shawls on her shoulders, and sat cross-legged in the chair across from the couch, looking much more like the woman who showed up an hour late to every family reunion with two bottles of wine for the adults and the best apple pie Talia's ever tasted.

"I pretend I see dead people for a living because really seeing them doesn't pay the bills," she said to Talia, all of twelve and very confused.

She told Talia about the spirit world, about the times of year and times of day and places on the map where the walls between the worlds were thin. She told Talia what she could expect going forward—how her power would develop, how she could use it to help people. She told Talia that most spirits just need a stern talking to, that very rarely was there a need for something as violent as an exorcism. Then she taught Talia how to perform an exorcism.

It was overwhelming to pre-teen Talia, but Rosa took her through it step by step, slowly and patiently over the years. She was always there if Talia had a question and she was happy to take Talia along on her various jaunts out into the world to help people who were being haunted. Talia didn't think of it as anything more than a weird hobby until she was a junior in college and her mother called her up to tell her that Rosa had died.

Ten minutes later, Rosa showed up to tell Talia herself.

Rosa stuck around the living world long enough to help Talia and her mother sort through Rosa's belongings, send things where they needed to go, and make sure her affairs were in order.

"You should keep my sign and phone line," she told Talia, shimmering from the window bench as Talia sorted through her paperwork. "It's good money."

"I don't need to pretend to be a psychic to make money, Aunt Rosa," Talia said with a sigh. "I can support myself without making people think I'm crazy."

"The thing about being a psychic is that anyone shrewd doesn't think you're crazy, they recognize that you're smart enough to make a quick buck off of the crazy ones."

Talia sighed again and Rosa rolled her eyes and that about summed up their relationship, even after death.

"At least keep my cell phone number," she said. "That's what the night job clients call, and if I'm not gonna be around, you're going to need a way to get in touch with them to help them out."

Talia doubted she'd be helping them out.

"And definitely keep Elijah."

"Who?" Talia asked, and Elijah flickered into view for the first time.

"Oh, good, you're an adult now," he said.

"Excuse me?"

"You were kind of annoying as a kid," he said. He was dressed in what she recognized from school as a Revolutionary War uniform. His hair was fair and long and tied back. He sounded bored. And unlike any depiction of colonial America she had ever seen before. Weren't they all supposed to have old-timey English accents?

"Elijah was haunting an old button that I found when I was a little older than you are now," Rosa said. "He's only a little annoying, so I keep him around. Kept him around. You know what I mean."

"It was a coat at one point," Elijah said. "The button is all that's left." He huffed. "As if I'd *choose* to haunt just a *button*. That's idiotic."

"You don't . . . sound the way you look," was all Talia could think to say.

"I've been a ghost for longer than this country has been a country," Elijah said. "You pick up some things. Speaking of, I hope you like *Law and Order* because I'm addicted and I'm going to be watching a lot of it if you take me home with you."

"What the hell?" Talia asked.

"You'll grow to love him," Rosa said.

"I sincerely doubt that," Talia said.

But she took Elijah anyway. And damn it if Rosa wasn't right.

Back in the present, she fumbles for her tablet on the coffee table so she can make sure she doesn't have any last minute appointments for the night job. In the end, she'd kept Rosa's cell phone after all, her good nature and inability to turn her back on someone in need of help at war with her desire to lead a normal life, apparently. A few years ago, the cell phone method was ditched for a simple website and it's worked out pretty well so far.

"I noticed you took the wrong coat this morning," Elijah says.

"It would have been nice if you'd mentioned that *before* I left the house," Talia says, stretching just far enough to close her fingers around the edge of her tablet case.

"I didn't realize it until after," he says. "Jesus, you're bitchy today."

"Like I said," she says. "A series of mistakes. Except—"

Mistake #18. She finishes that sentence.

"—there was this girl."

Elijah lights up immediately. Almost literally.

"A girl?" he asks.

"Just . . . you know . . . she paid for my coffee after I realized I didn't have my wallet," Talia says.

"Was she cute?"

"So cute that I don't understand why she was into me." Mistake number nineteen.

"She was *into you*?" Elijah asks gleefully. Goddamnit.

"Yes?" Talia says. "I mean, she asked me out. I mean—"

"You're going to get laid!" Elijah cheers.

"I think I'd like you better if you were stuck in the eighteenth century where people didn't talk about this shit," she mutters.

"Too bad, baby. They never should have invented television if they wanted ghosts to stay unchanging," Elijah says. "Don't even get me started on the internet."

Talia doesn't even have a chance to get him started on the internet, a subject which Elijah has been known to wax poetic about for hours despite the fact that the only person who can hear him is Talia and she really doesn't care. Her phone buzzes, interrupting him, and she nearly jumps a mile.

"World's most jittery exorcist," Elijah says.

"Shut up, E," Talia says absently as she looks down at the display. *Cute Anna from Starbucks* it says. Her heart leaps into her throat.

Mistake #20, just to round things out: she answers the phone without telling Elijah to scram or heading downstairs to the street and out of his haunting radius.

"Hello?"

"Talia?" says Anna. She even sounds bubbly and adorable over Talia's shitty cell phone connection. "It's Anna, from Starbucks?"

"Hi!" Talia says, because despite everyone in the world having caller ID, there's still this weird theatricality to answering a phone call like you don't know who's on the other end. "It's . . . nice to hear from you."

"I just got home," Anna says. "So I'd hoped you were home! And you are!" That's the sort of thing that would sound stilted and awkward if Talia said it, but sounds adorable coming out of Anna's mouth.

"I am," Talia says. "I got your text."

"Good! I was thinking, since it's Restaurant Week, we should totally take advantage and go to dinner."

Talia has only the vaguest idea of what Restaurant Week is, mostly garnered from watching *Top Chef* reruns with Elijah.

"That sounds great," Talia says. "I'd really—that would be great."

"I don't know if you have any preferences," Anna says, and Talia can hear her typing away. "I will tell you that I went to Sakura last Restaurant Week and the specials kind of suck and that I've been to Blue House Bistro and their food isn't worth it."

"No preferences," Talia says, because it's classier than admitting that she lives off take-out and things she can eat one-handed in her car.

"I'd love to try that new place on Dickerson Street, the one in the old church? I think it's called The Rectory? I know it's a little far outside of town, but I have a car and I'd be happy to drive."

"No, I have a car too," Talia says. She flips open her tablet and Googles *dickerson street church restaurant*. The Rectory's site pops up as the top search result and she clicks into it. Elijah appears over her shoulder—maybe she wouldn't be the world's most jittery medium if her goddamned ghost roommate would stay in one place—as the annoying flash splash page plays out. New dining experience, just converted from a church that's laid empty for decades, original interiors, blah blah blah, all sorts of stupid hipster crap that she doesn't care about, until finally she can click on a menu. She looks at it quickly, sees at least three or four things she likes and can afford, and then says, "I'm looking at it now, that seems great."

"Well, that place looks pretentious as hell," Elijah mutters. "I was actually around in the 1880s, you know, and it's not a look I think the world needs to recreate."

"Ssssh," she murmurs.

"Great!" Anna says. "I can make a reservation, then. Are you free tomorrow?"

"I'm just saying," Elijah continues, "Food-wise, architecture-wise, design-wise, they could do better."

Talia turns her head enough to glare at him as she pulls up her night job schedule in one tab and checks the site's inbox for new appointments in the other.

"Let me just check," she says. Nothing on the calendar. Nothing new in the inbox. "Yep, I'm definitely free."

"I can't believe you even had to check, it's not like you have any other friends," Elijah says.

"Shut up, E!" she hisses at him.

"What was that?" Anna asks.

"Nothing," Talia says quickly, "Just talking to my . . . roommate."

"'Roommate,'" Elijah repeats with air quotes. The twenty-first century has completely ruined what was probably once a kind and cordial colonial gentleman.

Talia covers the bottom of her phone with her hand and hisses, "I will exorcise the shit out of you if you don't shut *up*."

Elijah raises his hands and fades out of existence again and Talia sighs and refocuses on the phone.

"Anyway, sorry about that, I sent him packing," she says. "Tomorrow night sounds great. Thursday is a design day, not a client day, so I'm free whenever you're ready."

"Let me see what time I can get a reservation for and I'll text you?" she says.

"That would be awesome," Talia says. "I'm really looking forward to—"

On Anna's side of the phone there's an obnoxiously loud ringing.

"Oh, crap," she says. "That's my work phone. I've gotta go—I'll text you though! And I hate to cut this off, I'd love to talk more, but at least we have tomorrow night!"

"I'm excited about it," Talia says, and hopes that sounds sincere.

"Me too," Anna says. "Talk to you later!"

Talia says goodbye and hangs up just as she hears Anna yell, "Shush, shush, I'm coming!" to the other phone, which is kind of adorable. She sighs and leans back against the couch, tablet on her knees, phone against her chest. After a moment, Elijah reappears.

"Wow, you're already pretty into this girl," he says.

"Well, she's a pretty girl who likes me," Talia says. "That alone is worth the effort. She's really—I don't know. I don't know what it is about her. Something about her just . . . clicked."

"How long did you talk this morning?" Elijah asks.

"Hardly at all! About half an hour over coffee and then I had to run. I barely know her. And she's cute, but that's not it, I felt . . . drawn to her? I guess? It was weird. She was weird. Adorable, but, like. . ."

"Babe, you talk to ghosts," Elijah says. "Was she 'talks to ghosts' weird, or—?"

"No, no," Talia says. "Not like that. 'Cute' weird, not 'constantly irritated by strangers no one else can see' weird. Just, really open and cheerful and she didn't even hesitate to say hi and flirt and talk to me and get me to talk about myself. I've never met anyone like that before."

"So, she has normal human feelings and reactions, then?" Elijah asks. "Super weird, yeah, I feel that."

A lot of people in Talia's underground network of mediums and exorcists have been working towards a way to touch ghosts. Talia really wants them to hurry up so she can smack Elijah when he deserves it.

"I don't know!" Talia says. She throws her hands up in the air. "I date other totally awkward people! I don't date normal people! Mostly because I know eventually I'm going to have to . . . tell them things."

Something like sympathy passes over Elijah's face.

"You should take my button with you so I can scope her out," he says, a not-so-delicate subject change. She appreciates it nonetheless.

"Nope," she says. "I'll tell you about it after. The last thing I need is you whispering in my ear all night and making me look crazier than usual."

"You never let me have any fun," he says with a sigh worthy of a twenty-first century diva, not an eighteenth century soldier. "Anyway, you should eat dinner and then we should start getting caught up with all the *Criminal Minds* on the DVR."

Food that isn't granola bars and mindless television sounds like exactly what she needs after a day full of exhausting mistakes. This is a first date with a girl she's known for a day. She doesn't need to worry about explaining her weird abilities or her weird night job or her weird roommate. Tonight, she can zone out and relax. If tomorrow goes well, then maybe she can start figuring out the easiest way to introduce someone to her world.

"I'll order pizza," she says, and makes herself comfortable on the couch as the television and cable box turn on by an invisible hand.

Dickerson Street winds from downtown all the way through the outskirts of cheap student housing, past the university, and into the suburbs. Talia's been up and down it probably about five thousand times since she got her driver's license, but she's never noticed the old church set back from the road that's been recently converted into a restaurant. As she turns off the road, she sees why—the bushes and trees have been hacked away and obviously used to shield it from the street. The vegetation that's left has been meticulously shaped to line the driveway down to the newly paved parking lot. The lot is small but mostly full and the church itself still looks like it was built at the turn of the last century, even with the addition of electric lights.

Talia parks and checks her make up one final time in the mirror, then heads up to the entrance. She can see Anna already waiting outside and she can't help but blush and grin at the sight of her.

She's not going to screw this up. She's not going to talk about a) ghosts; b) the spirit world; c) arcane trivia she's picked up from Elijah; d) Elijah in general, because that has the potential to get too weird too quickly; e) most of her hobbies; f) ancient religious rituals; g) her night job; or h) her stupid succulents, god, why did she bring them up at Starbucks? She's going to be normal. She's going to be cute. She's going to be someone that you would definitely want to go on a second date with. She's not going to be weird.

"Talia!" Anna says as soon as Talia is within shouting distance. "You look amazing!"

Elijah picked out Talia's outfit after an entire afternoon of psyching herself out. She's wearing a navy blue lace dress and grey flats; they're the nicest non-black things she owns. Anna, on the other hand, is rocking a green dress with navy polka dots. She's wearing cute heels. Her hair is in some sort of elaborate knot on her head. Her red lipstick is to die for. She looks perfect and that weird pull that Talia's felt since the start sparks brightly in her chest.

"You do too," Talia manages to say in a normal voice, not a squeak or a mumble, thank god. Maybe she can pull off this normal date thing after all.

She clings to that thought for about half a minute until they step inside the restaurant and it all goes to hell.

The back of her neck prickles. Her ears ring a little. The air in the room shifts. Fuck. There's a ghost in the restaurant.

She tries not to panic as Anna chats with the hostess and they're lead to a table. There are ghosts lots of places. Most ghosts aren't harmful at all and many of them don't bother messing with the living. Many of them will fade out completely when they notice a medium on the premise, stealing back into the spirit world until the coast is clear and they know they won't be exorcised. Most ghosts that do make themselves known can be talked into calming down and ending any disturbances they're causing. There's no reason to panic.

103

That doesn't stop Talia from panicking.

The hostess hands them both the Restaurant Week menus and rattles off a list of drink specials. Talia had hoped to have a glass of wine to calm her nerves, but. Well. Probably better to skip, just in case.

"Do you want to get a bottle of wine?" Anna asks, as if she's a very bad mind reader.

"I shouldn't," Talia says. "Wine makes me . . . " There are a million ways she can end this sentence that aren't weird. " . . . irritable." Crap. That definitely isn't one of them. "But, uh, you go ahead."

"Well, I'm hoping to keep you in a good mood, so I'm gonna take a pass," Anna says. Her eyes are still sparkling a little with the good humor Talia remembers from yesterday morning. Maybe this date is still salvageable. Maybe Talia just needs to take a deep breath.

"So," she says, forcing herself to smile like a normal person, "have you read any reviews of this place? What's supposed to be good?"

"I haven't, yet," Anna says. "I think it just opened like, last week. But general word-of-mouth seems to be that it's pretty great. I'm thinking the pork chop sounds good, and the stuffed chicken? I'm a sucker for goat cheese."

"Who isn't?" Talia says in the hopes it will make Anna smile again and—yes!—it definitely does. "The pork chop sounds good. God, it's been forever since I've been out to a real restaurant." Does that make her sound like a hermit? "Just, you know. Work keeps me busy." Her work where she sets her own hours. Shit. "And. Life."

Anna rolls with it. "Yeah, I hate eating alone too. I mean, the actual act of eating alone is fine, but people get so freaking judgey! Especially as a fat chick. You wouldn't believe the things people have the gall to say to total strangers!"

Talia abruptly wants to find those people and—well, she's not great with violence, but maybe glare at them for a while.

"People are assholes," Talia agrees. "What the fuck. It's none of their business."

"Exactly!" Anna says, and folds her hands on top of the table, as if she's proved her point. Talia is absolutely going to kiss her before the night is over. Anna clears her throat and looks a little flustered for the first time all night. "Sorry, I have a lot of feelings about body shaming. Um, anyway, my job keeps me out a lot of nights, so I don't get to eat out as much as I'd like given how many great places there are in the city. That's why I love Restaurant Week. I can cram six months of foodie-ing it up into a week and then not feel as guilty about eating at the same three places the rest of the time."

"I don't even go *out* to the same three places, I just get take-out," Talia admits. "I—"

And then the lights flicker.

Lights flicker all the time. In an old building like this even new electric lines are probably twisted up. There are a million and one reasons for the lights to hiccup.

But throw in the buzz in the air directly before the flicker, the static electricity that's suddenly filling the room, and the very particular whine that rings out right before they flick back on, and it very quickly gets narrowed down to one reason. One terrible, shitty, date-ruining reason.

Anna is saying something, commenting on the lights, Talia thinks, on the way the temperature of the room just dropped, but Talia is focused on the room, on looking around for the source of the disturbance, looking for anything out of the ordinary. She can't see anything obvious, which means she's going to have to call it to her. Great.

When she looks back at Anna, she's looking at Talia expectantly. She must have just asked a question. Crap.

"Um, I'm just going to—just, find the bathroom?" Talia stands up a little too quickly and Anna's eyes widen in alarm. Oh god, she probably thinks Talia's running away to puke her guts out or something equally gross. "I'll be right back!"

She hustles away from the table, grabbing her bag as she goes. Shit. She almost didn't bring this stuff with her, but it's probably good that she did. It would have been harder to come up with an excuse to run out to the car than it is to leave the table temporarily.

The hallway housing the restrooms is small, narrow, and empty. Thankfully. Talia fumbles in her bag for a pouch of chalk dust and glances around quickly, looking for a place to draw the appropriate symbols where they won't be noticed. There's a table that casts just enough shadow on the wall to cover a large enough area to get to work, so she drops to her knees and smudges the runes into place as quickly as possible.

"You who dwell between here and beyond, make yourself—"

"I'm *here*, no need for all of that."

Talia just barely swallows her shout of surprise. She spills chalk dust on the ground and, unfortunately, on her skirt. She knows from experience that it's going to be a bitch to get it off the lace.

She gets to her feet and turns to confront the ghost, hands on her hips. The ghost is maybe in her forties and dressed for the time period the church was last used in, the turn of the twentieth century. She also looks displeased.

"Look," Talia says. "I don't want to make this a thing. I'm here for dinner, not for an exorcism. What do you need? Why are you bothering people?"

"I'm *not*," the ghost says. "There's something here, something buried in the walls. It's been here for years, it's the reason I'm still here. I thought you were here to help me, finally!"

"What?" Talia asks. She's heard a lot of excuses from ghosts before. This is a new one. "Please, lady, I swear, I'll leave you alone if you just leave me alone for the next few hours, okay?"

"I'm not doing any of this!" the ghost insists. "There's something here, you have to help me!"

Talia raises a single eyebrow and crosses her arms. This isn't the first time a reckless spirit has tried to con her into something.

"I'm telling the truth!"

"Look—what's your name?" Talia asks.

"Martha," the ghost says flatly.

"Martha," Talia says. "I'm serious. I'm here on a dinner date. I'm not coming after you. Just leave these people alone for the next couple hours and I swear I'll come back tomorrow and we can talk this out and figure out what you need. I just really, really don't have time for it now."

"I'm not. Doing. This."

"Then all these things are going to stop, right? When I go back and finish my dinner? Because you're not doing anything?" She's probably been gone too long already, Anna is probably wondering what's taking her so long.

"You're not listening to me!" Martha snaps.

"You're not telling me anything worth listening to!" Talia says. "Lights flickering? Static charge? Other-worldly noise? Temperature fluctuation? This is textbook ghost shit, Martha. I've been doing this since

I was twelve years old; I can tell when something is being haunted and I've met too many ghosts who swear up and down they're not the ones causing the disturbances to buy into your shit. Cut it out for the next few hours and I'll help you live out your dying request or get revenge on whomever or visit your descendants or listen to you talk about whatever's on your mind."

"You're *useless*!" Martha whispers, and disappears in a flash.

Talia has a sinking suspicion that she just egged Martha onto upping her game instead of cutting it out, but maybe she'll get lucky. Maybe Martha will see how amazing Anna looks and give Talia a break.

Yeah, right. Not likely.

Talia rushes back to the table with the big fake smile plastered on her face. Anna is frowning as she checks her phone, glancing occasionally around the room.

"*So* sorry about that," Talia says. "Anyway . . . I think I'm going to go with the pork chop after all."

"Great," Anna says, but she still seems distracted. "I need to check in really quick with my dog sitter, I'll be right back, okay?"

She doesn't even look at Talia as she gets up and heads towards the front door, eyes glued to her phone. Great. The meal hasn't even started yet and already Talia has put Anna off. This is why she can't have nice things.

Talia spends Anna's absence watching the room like a hawk for further signs of paranormal disturbance. The lights stay on and the room stays the right temperature and no one starts screaming in horror and nothing moves by itself. Martha doesn't reappear, and Talia thinks maybe, *maybe* everything is going to be okay after all.

She doesn't have to fake her smile when Anna returns.

"Sorry about that," Anna says when she takes her seat again. She really does look sorry. "Fig was acting weird and the dog-sitter thought he ate something. You know how it goes."

"Totally," Talia says and hopes she sounds like a person who tolerates animals. "So, what's Fig like?"

"Oh, he's great!" Anna says, animated again. "He's this big mutt, but he's smart and sweet and I couldn't ask for a better friend, you know? I know it's really cheesy to call animals your friends, but we really have this weird bond." She pulls out her phone and shows Talia the lockscreen, which is definitely a picture of a big fluffy dog-like thing. Definitely a mutt. Talia's never seen anything quite like it before.

"Awww, he looks sweet," she lies. Animals are definitely not her thing.

"He's the sweetest," Anna says, and peers down lovingly at him before she replaces her phone on the table. Face up. Talia hopes that's not a bad sign.

The waiter reappears to take their order and Talia's barely considered the menu. She goes with the pork chop, because it's literally the only thing she can remember and her eyes won't focus on the words any longer. When he clears out, Anna folds her hands on the table again and smiles and Talia forces herself to calm down and breathe like a normal human and let herself relax.

"So," Anna says. "How long have you lived in—"

The lights go again and Talia swears out loud a little more fervently than is called for. Anna must think she's afraid of the dark. When the lights come back, it's with a distant echoing smash. Talia leans out of her seat; every single sconce on the wall leading to the kitchen has fallen to the floor. There's no such thing as a coincidence in a place with a ghost. Shit.

While Anna is still peering at the broken sconces, concerned, Talia slides open her phone and maneuvers to a place where she can force a text alert out of it. When it buzzes, she picks it up with feigned concern.

"Oh, no," she says. "I'm so sorry, it's Elijah, my roommate. He's . . . having a bit of a cooking disaster. He needs my help." She forces a laugh. "I'd just ignore him, but the last time he set the kitchen on fire, so. . ." She gives what she hopes is a properly apologetic smile and then rushes back to the restroom hallway.

"*Martha*!" she hisses as soon as she's sure she's alone. Martha appears immediately.

"If you're just going to yell at me, I'm leaving," she warns Talia. "You don't understand what it's like here! It's been me and that *thing* for hundreds of years! I can't properly see it, I can't properly interact with it, it's just *there*. It's there and it's cold and it won't let me go and it's tied to this place—the priests did something, it was in the wall—I don't know, but you have to believe me!"

Talia hesitates for the barest moment. Martha's taking this whole thing pretty far. It's possible she's telling the truth.

Except, Occam's Razor, right? She's been doing the ghost thing for years, her aunt was doing it for longer, and the thing that Martha is describing sounds like no ghost Talia's ever encountered or even read about. It sounds like the sort of story someone might make up after years on their own, locked away in an abandoned church, bored out of their skull.

"Martha, I'm serious," Talia says. "Cut it the hell out! I hate performing exorcisms and I know you guys don't like them either. I know they tear you apart. I don't want to do that to you! I'm a firm believer in ghosts and the living coexisting peacefully." She narrows her eyes. "But I swear to god, if this girl dumps me because you're bored and want to fuck around with a medium on her night off, I will send you back to the spirit world so hard your damn ancestors will feel it!"

She turns on hell and stalks back to the table before Martha can say anything else. A cold creature keeping her hostage. Yeah right. If nothing else, whatever was hidden would have been pretty quickly unhidden when they gutted the church to turn it into a restaurant, right?

"Sorry, sorry," Talia says, slipping back into her seat. "God, he's a handful. I wish I could afford to live alone, but you know how it goes, you've gotta take whatever Craigslist throws at you. I feel like I'm ruining the night, running back and forth."

"It's fine, it's fine, seriously," Anna says. "Don't worry about it—these things happen." The way she's scanning the room for an exit belies the ease of her words. She literally looks like she's trying to find a way to escape, which only makes sense considering how consistently Talia's blown her off this evening. It's a wonder she's still sitting here. Talia isn't surprised that she keeps surreptitiously checking her phone and frowning. She's probably texting her friends about what a rude flake her date is.

"I can make it up to you," Talia says. "I swear, maybe we can go get coffee or something after this? I'll turn my phone off and everything."

"That'd be great," Anna says, but she's still frowning down at her lap. Talia can see the glow from the screen on her phone. Talia's blown it already.

So, it's really just inevitable that the lights go again. The sound is louder this time, and the static electricity literally crackles around them. The rest of the diners only seem vaguely distracted, but they don't know the signs. They weren't taught to look for these things wherever they go. This isn't the damn job that they never asked for in the first place.

She sighs and pinches the bridge of her nose, then fakes another text.

"Oh, god, it's Elijah again," Talia lies. "I hate to do this to you—it's so embarrassing, I'm going to kill him later, but I don't want him to set the kitchen on fire again—I'll be right back, and this will be the last time, I swear."

Anna smiles, but it seems a little forced and she's still distracted by her phone. Fuck, Talia is bombing this date with one of the most alluring, beautiful girls who's ever been interested in her. She's going to exorcise Martha out of spite.

She taps her phone screen a few times, pretending to call someone, then presses the phone against her ear and walks back to the bathroom hallway. Once she's out of sight, she shoves the phone back into her bag and hisses, "*Martha!*"

Martha looks pissed when she reappears, but she's got nothing on Talia.

"Do you understand what is happening here?" Talia all but shouts before Martha can open her mouth. "I'm trying to live my fucking life! I've been a medium for almost twenty years and it somehow fucks me over again and again and all I want is like, a person! A person who can hold my hand and hug me and rub my shoulders after a hard day! All I want is someone who lights up when they see me! I have a best friend who's a ghost and a house full of fucking plants and sometimes not having human contact *sucks*, so I get it! I get what it's like to feel all alone! I get that the afterlife sucks! And I can help you work through whatever shit you need to work through, but I need to do it *tomorrow!*"

"You're not listening!" Martha shouts, and the lights flicker ominously again. Talia glares at her.

"See?" she says. "That's the sort of shit I'm talking about! How can you stand there and pretend it's not you doing this?"

"Okay, well, that time it was me," Martha allows. "But the rest—I'm not the one doing it, it's that . . . that *thing!*"

"Right," Talia says. "The monster that lives here. That no one else sees or interacts with. That just happens to be doing all the usual ghostly doings."

"Maybe they're not just ghostly doings!" Martha says. "Maybe other things do it too! Because I'm *sorry* you don't have someone to hug and cuddle with, but I've spent two hundred years not being able to interact with *anything*, enslaved to some sort of creature, watching the caretaker's television through his window at the end of the day! Your loneliness has nothing on me, lady, and for the last time, *I need your help!*"

The lights flicker again.

"Right," Talia says.

"That one wasn't me!" Martha insists, and Talia is tired of all of this.

"This is your last warning, Martha," Talia says, lowering her voice. "I have enough stuff in my bag to do a proper exorcism and if this doesn't stop, fuck my date, I'll do it right here and now and you can cry about it to your friends in the spirit world."

"You *bitch!*" Martha says, but Talia ignores her and stomps back out towards the table, aware that her face is red and her hands are shaking and she looks a mess and she has completely ruined this date.

"Sorry, sorry," she says breathlessly as she slips back into her seat, smoothing her hair down. "Just, you know, Elijah. Ha. So . . . bad at cooking. Needs my help with everything." She clears her throat. "Anyway, you were saying?"

Anna isn't looking at her, though, Anna is looking down at her phone still, distracted.

"Oh, I just need to . . . take this call," Anna says. She flashes Talia a big smile, but it's not as sincere as it should be and Talia feels her heart sink. She ruined it. This totally awesome girl and she sunk her own chances at a second date with this stupid ghost bullshit. She's going to exorcise this goddamn ghost to death if it's the last thing she does.

She touches Anna's wrist before she can stand up again. Better to be the better person and rip the Band-Aid off at once than sit through the rest of an awkward meal with someone who obviously isn't into her anymore.

"Look, Anna, I get it. It's okay. If this isn't working for you, it's not working for you. It happens. We can just—"

Before she can finish the rest of her "I know it's not you, it's definitely me, sorry I'm a weirdo" speech, there's a sharp scream somewhere behind her. She turns around as another person screams, and suddenly there's a mob of waiters and kitchen staff pouring out of the kitchen in a panic, which is making the diners panic, which is whipping the room up into a frenzy. She can hear smashes and crashes from the kitchen and that static buzz is turned up to eleven. Just fucking great.

She lets go of Anna's wrist and jumps to her feet, grabbing her bag and stomping through the hysterical crowd towards the kitchen.

"I'm going to exorcise you *so hard,* you *asshole!*" she shouts, heedless of the frantic diners around her. She slams open the swinging doors to the kitchen, chalk dust already in hand, and then—

Freezes.

Because. The thing in the kitchen. The thing in the kitchen is not a ghost.

"What the—" she starts to say, but the thing, whatever it is, ten feet tall and black as night, black as anything, black itself, really, an absence in the shape of something pointed and sharp and thin, catches sight of her. A volley of knives heads straight towards her and thank god years of exorcisms have honed those fight-or-flight instincts, because she hits the ground and rolls behind a counter before they can hit her.

"See! I told you! I told you!" Martha says, appearing at her side. "It's not me, it wasn't me, I don't know what it is, it's evil and it keeps me here and it's *cold,* it's the only thing I've felt since I died, the coldness—"

"*Shut up!*" Talia hisses and crawls across the floor. The ceiling above them is cracking, but plaster and paint aren't raining down—the cracks are like the thing itself, dark and inky and deep, there and not, like peering into something else, into *nothing* else. She feels cold, too. She can see the thing from between the shelves of the counter. It reminds her of an Ent, but smaller, tall and thin and jagged with long, twisting limbs. It has no face, no features, the whole thing is just *blackness.* She's overcome by the urge to throw up, but she has to focus. She fumbles for the chalk dust. An exorcism might not work, but it's the only tool she's got.

"Get the fuck out of here, Martha, if you don't want to be sent back," she says, her voice shaking. She pours herself a handful of chalk dust and starts chanting, the words steady even as her body shakes. *You-who-*

dwell-between-here-and-beyond-between-worlds-unbidden-between-life-and-death—

The doors swing open again and this time Talia does stutter. Because it's Anna.

And she's *glowing.*

The black thing froze when the doors hit the walls and there's a roaring in Talia's ears, a painful, angry sound that she can't describe, a sound that she can feel in her bones. She wants to cover her ears, but she knows that won't stop it. Anna doesn't seem to hear it, or maybe it doesn't affect her. She's chanting too, shouting, really, a green aura around her as foreign words spill from her lips. It's no language Talia can recognize and something tells her it's ancient or secret, something not for her ears. Anna doesn't even look at her, walking steadily towards the blackness, her arms held straight out in front of her, palms out. The sound gets louder, fiercer, worse, and Talia has to double over, wrapping her arms around her head. Her brain is going to explode. Her *body* is going to explode. Whatever is happening is happening to Martha too— there's agony on her face and she's not disappearing or escaping or moving, just frozen where she stood next to Talia.

And then, just as sudden as the noise came, it stops.

Talia blinks open her eyes and stays frozen for a moment, curled in the fetal position. Her ears ring in the sudden silence and she stumbles up to her feet.

The blackness is gone. The cracks in the ceiling are gone. The kitchen is a mess, but it's empty except for her, Anna, and Martha. Anna is breathing hard, flushed and angry and Talia probably shouldn't find her so attractive after what just happened but she can't help it.

"I told you it wasn't me," Martha mutters again, breaking the moment. Anna turns around to stare at them with wide eyes. Talia pinches the bridge of her nose.

"Yes, okay, it wasn't you, Jesus, Martha, go back to doing whatever the fuck it is you were doing," Talia says.

"No need to be so rude," Martha says with a huff, and then promptly disappears. Talia looks heavenward and then closes her eyes. When she opens them again, Anna is walking hesitantly towards her. Her dress is rumpled and her hair has fallen down. She's still so beautiful Talia can't handle it.

"Was that a ghost?" she asks tentatively.

"Yeah," Talia says. She rubs the back of her neck. "That's where I've been rushing off to all night. I thought all the weird things that were happening were because of her, but it turns out she was telling the truth—it was that . . . thing, instead."

"We call it a Void," Anna says. "It's, um, sort of a thing from another dimension that wants to turn our dimension inside out to bring theirs front and center? It's hard to explain. I mostly focus on getting rid of them."

"So you're a. . ." Talia doesn't know how she was planning on ending that sentence. She has no idea what Anna could possibly be.

"Conjurer," Anna says. "Well, I mostly reverse-conjure stuff that long-ago conjurers accidently unleashed on the world." She's either flushed from the exertion or blushing. "My three-greats-ago grandfather was head of the Conjurers Guild on the east coast, there was this thing, it all fell apart . . . it's a long story, but those of us who are left with the ability try to undo what went wrong, basically."

"Wow," is all Talia can think to say. Anna stops walking. She's an arm's length away, now.

"And you're . . . an exorcist?"

"That's . . . not really the term, but yeah," Talia says. "A medium, I guess? I can converse with spirits. Most of the time there's no exorcism necessary, but sometimes violent or confused spirits need to be forcibly sent back to the spirit world."

Anna nods like that's a perfectly reasonable explanation.

"So, all the running around was because you thought you needed to do an exorcism?" she says. "Not because you thought our date was tedious? Because all my running around was definitely trying to figure out if there really was a Void here and where it was and how best to get rid of it. I'm sorry if you thought I wasn't into you."

"Apology accepted," Talia says absently. "I'm really into you. So."

Anna smiles slowly. "Good. I was afraid you would think I was weird."

"Well, you are," Talia says. "But it's 'cute' weird, not 'being irritated by things other people generally can't see' weird. Because that's really my status quo. Ghosts are annoying little shits."

"Same with demons," Anna says. "And they *ruin* my night life."

"Absolutely true," Talia says, smiling slowly. "And it's hardly the weirdest thing about me. I mix mayonnaise and ketchup for my French fries and I sleep with my socks on. Also, I totally lied up and down yesterday morning, I don't normally drink coffee and I think it's pretty gross, I just needed the caffeine because I'd been out talking to a particularly annoying ghost all night."

Anna makes a face. "Ugh, okay, the mayonnaise thing might be a deal breaker. I don't care about the ghosts, but that's gross. But I can put up with that if you can put up with the fact that I like to dip potato chips in cottage cheese."

The disgusted face Talia makes in response to that is completely involuntary, but it makes Anna laugh.

"Way weirder than the demon thing," Talia says.

"And my dog is . . . maybe not so much a dog as some sort of dog-like creature I found around a dimensional anomaly," Anna admits. "He's still sweet and house-trained, though!"

"That's okay, Elijah's not so much my roommate as he's a ghost that haunts a button I inherited," she says.

"A button?" Anna asks.

"Well, he used to haunt a coat . . . it's a long story."

Anna smiles at her and she full on swoons.

"I can't wait to hear it," she says, reaching out to take Talia's hand. "Do you want to go to the diner and get an actual dinner and talk about it?"

"Definitely," Talia says.

Interdimensional destruction be damned, this is definitely the best date Talia's ever had.

Shadow

Lara Eckener

Worship is most dour in a haunted house,
it doesn't matter who is lord inside. There's
a blackness in the walls reaching out,
stretching across flagstone so recently liberated
from thick red carpet, a turn of the century opulence
we never quite got used to.

Me, the shiver down your spine, the reflection
you almost caught in the mirror. It, something else,
that feeling that hits in the middle of the night
when you're laughing alone and realize
mid-inhale, that one day you won't be here
to laugh anymore. I used to laugh. I used to—

In one ear the priests from a century ago theologize
about the time their congregation might have left.
In the other, polished people with
flippant manners and disrespectful tones
talk about the time they have left.

In these bodies,
in this temple,
in that horror the ritual bound me to,
life after life after life.
It's not as silent as they promised.

Out of Uniform

Christine Ricketts

It began as many nonuniform strips of dyed cloth, like a puzzle that had yet to be put together. (Though in actuality, it began as coarse fur on the backs of sheep and from stalks of a fibrous plant growing tall, but that's a bit more detail than this story really needs.) Strong and nimble fingers plucked up each piece of cloth and carefully stitched it into its proper place, guided by pattern, skill, and a thriving need for independence. Maybe the stitches were not perfectly straight, and perhaps there would be a bit of a pinch in the shoulders but the color (blue with red facing) and the cut would be enough to distinguish the wearer across the smoky chaos of a battlefield. And the young chap who tugged it over his hunting shirt would know immediately that he belonged to the single most important movement of the century.

The Revolution.

Elijah hurried down North Marlborough Street, doing his best not to push through the meandering crowds of people headed to and from the markets, or the shops, or visits or just random afternoon walks that caused them to be directly in the space he was trying to move through. He had a purpose, a very specific purpose, a very specific and *important* purpose that needed to be seen to *post haste*. Unless he wanted to be on the receiving end of a verbal thrashing by Sergeant Whitt for being what the oft red-faced, walking bull-horn considered "out of uniform."

He most definitely did not want to be so blessed.

Besides, missing one—he raised an arm to check his cuff—or two buttons hardly seemed like enough to be out of uniform. He had the coat itself, did he not? As well as the shirt, the waistcoat, the sturdy trousers, and boots that very nearly fit. All bought and paid for properly—except for the boots. Those he had nicked from Drunk Tom who had been, well, drunk and therefore hardly in need of his boots, which likely weren't his to begin with. And anyway the lousy sot had certainly cheated him at cards more than once and so owed Elijah the favor. In a roundabout way.

All he needed now was a tailor. Any halfway decent clothier should be able to reattach a button—or two—in less time than it would take Sergeant Whitt to notice an untucked bib. And once that minor deed was accomplished, Elijah would be free to join his friends at the Grapes to raise as many tankards as they could manage in the hours before dawn. There was a battle promised for the morning that he was becoming certain would look more promising with the help of good, strong beer.

He was nearly at the end of the street before he saw the slightly faded sign with "tailor" carved into it. Bearing down on his impatience—the Grapes was not very likely to run out of ale—he maneuvered his way around a group of slow-moving ladies, pausing, of course, to tip his hat, then pulled up short just as a horse and cart nearly ran him down. He gave a flick of his hand to the back of the driver before straightening his jacket and ducking through the open doorway of the dressmaker.

The shop was small; just a few feet in from the door was a long, waist-high counter. Behind it were shelves of fabric neatly folded and stacked atop each other. To the right was a closed curtain, presumably leading back to another room. Presently the shop appeared empty, though Elijah thought he could hear the sounds of rustling nearby. That could have been coming from outside; it was difficult to tell. On the counter was a small bell with an equally small hammer next to it. With barely a thought he snatched up the hammer and before the ring had time to fade from the air the curtain slid open.

Once, when Elijah had been ten, he had fallen from the upper branches of an oak tree—a good fifteen feet from the ground. He somewhat recalled the brief sensation of weightlessness as he had fallen, the swoop in his stomach. What he more vividly remembered was the hard, sudden shock of hitting the ground and the way it had driven the breath from his lungs.

Strange to find that the exact same feeling could occur minus the falling from a tree bit.

The young man that stepped in from behind the curtain had chestnut-colored hair swept back from his face, which was sharply angled and with a complexion more fitted to a nobleman than a working lad. He wore a pristine white shirt far more elegant than the one Elijah had pulled over his head that morning, and the young man's vest was a deep green fabric with a soft texture that Elijah had never even seen before. It looked like something one would see at a fancy ball or party—if one were invited to fancy balls or parties.

And when did you become an expert in clothing and fancy parties? a voice inside his head asked, as the young man's eyes met his. Even they were an odd mixture of blue and green that looked exotic.

"Hello," the young man greeted with a smile and a slight nod of his head. "How may I help you?"

Elijah blinked. "What?" he asked dumbly. His head felt like it were stuffed full of cotton.

The young man's eyebrows lifted, but the rest of his expression remained the same. "How may I help you?" he repeated, an extra bit of lift in the end of the question.

Elijah blinked again and looked around the shop. He suddenly could not remember what he was doing there. Shelves of fabric. A dressmaker dummy in the corner. A tall mirror next to it. He glanced down at himself; on the red facing of his coat—on the left side—was an empty space where a silver button should have been. His head lifted.

"Button," he blurted out. In his mind he saw a smaller version of himself, only that version was holding his head in his hands as if it were in danger of falling off completely.

The young man tipped his head to the right. His eyes dropped to the empty space on Elijah's jacket. "You require a new button?" he guessed.

Elijah nodded. "Yes." Then shook his head. "No. That is, I mean . . ." he trailed off and reached both hands into the pockets of his trousers. Empty. Removing them, he checked the pockets in his coat. The left side was empty as well. But in the right side pocket his fingers closed over something small and metal. Pulling his hand free, he held his arm out to the tailor, palm open. The button sat in the center.

"I have a button," he declared. The small version of himself in his mind covered its face with its hands.

The tailor's smile widened just a fraction. "And you need it to be sewn back on?"

Elijah considered the question. Then he realized he was considering for much, much longer than was necessary. He nodded, his arm still stretched out in front of him. "Yes."

Bobbing his head, the tailor plucked the button from Elijah's hand. "Well, that's simple enough. If you'll remove your coat, I can replace it for you now."

Withdrawing his arm, Elijah brought his hands together, pressing the thumb of his left hand into the palm of his right. The tailor's fingers had barely brushed his skin and the whole of his hand tingled. An almost echoing sensation was working up the base of his spine. How odd.

He raised his gaze to find the tailor looking at him expectantly. His hands squeezed together reflexively. "Yes?" he asked.

The tailor motioned with one hand. "Your coat?"

Elijah gave a sharp exhale and shook himself slightly. "Right. Of course." He shrugged the coat back off his shoulders and then wiggled madly for a moment to get it to slide down to his hands. The left side came easily enough but the right side remained stubbornly in place until he tugged on it with his free hand. He started to hand the coat over and then hesitated. It felt oddly heavy, as if he were passing over something much more than a piece of stitched fabric.

With an easy movement the tailor scooped it into his hands and spread it over the counter. He drew forth a needle and a piece of thread, almost like a magician in a passing carnival. As Elijah watched, the tailor made several quick, neat stitches, pulled the thread, knotted it tightly and then snipped it with a pair of scissors in what seemed like the same motion. He tugged lightly on the button and appeared satisfied by the resistance he felt. His hands brushed down over the front of the coat and then paused.

"Oh. But it appears you're missing another?" he pointed out.

Elijah, who had been a bit saddened by how quickly the process had transpired, followed the point of the tailor's finger. At the right cuff were three buttons followed by an empty space and a few dangling threads.

"I must have lost it on my way here," he replied, a sinking feeling in his stomach. He did not bother checking his pockets; he knew it would not be there. The tailor leaned forward to examine the other buttons on the coat.

"Hmmm. I do not believe that I have anything that would match these." Reaching underneath the counter, the tailor brought forth a large tray filled with odd bits and baubles. As his long fingers rummaged through, Elijah could see that there was nothing that looked remotely like the missing button. And he could just imagine Sergeant Whitt's response to seeing a mismatched piece of uniform.

"However, I believe I know where I might find some. It may take a bit of time, though," the tailor offered.

Elijah scratched at his chin thoughtfully. "I'm meeting some friends at the Grapes. I could return in a few hours?" he stated.

To his surprise, the tailor smiled again, wider and warmer than before. "How fortunate! It happens that I have business at the Grapes this evening. When I have finished with your coat, I could bring it to you there?" he suggested.

The sinking feeling reversed itself so quickly that Elijah nearly choked on it. Instead he swallowed down the flutters trying to climb up his throat and felt his own smile tug at the corners of his mouth.

"I—yes—that would be . . . nice," he finished. "Thank you," he added quickly.

"Oh, you're most welcome Master . . .?" The tailor's question hung in the air for a moment before Elijah understood what he was asking.

"Oh, Elijah. My name is Elijah Connelly. But Elijah will do."

"Elijah, then. It is a pleasure to meet you." The tailor held out a hand. Elijah clasped it firmly and felt an arrow of sensation shoot up his arm.

"And you are?" he heard himself asked as they shook. And even as they released their grips, their eyes held, grey to greenish blue.

"Matthew. Matthew Cutter."

Matthew Cutter.

Seated comfortably, or as comfortable as one could get on a rickety stool, at the bar of the Bunch of Grapes Tavern, Elijah wondered if the tailor bore any relations to George Cutter. He squinted, but could not really see any resemblance to the dock-worker's rough, hangdog face. In addition, George was a tosser and a git, two terms which he could not imagine being applied to Mister Matthew Cutter.

Matthew. He leaned upon his hand and wordlessly mouthed the name to himself, feeling an echo of that shivery sensation he had felt before in the shop. Matthew. It was a pleasing name. Biblical.

Like mine, he thought, smiling slightly.

There was an abrupt thump as a hand slammed down on the bar beside him, startling Elijah out of his reverie. His head swiveled to the right and he found himself looking into the grinning, oft-punched face of Billy Boyle. He was bracing himself even as Billy's hand lifted from the bar top and fell, with nearly as much force, against Elijah's back. The energy traveled down through his body and his feet kicked out against the bottom of the bar.

"Elijah! Jus' the man I was hopin' to find!" Billy announced loudly. He did everything loudly. He held up one hand and Elijah winced but it was only to signal to the barkeep at the other side of the room. While the barkeep made his way over, Billy grabbed hold of Elijah's tankard and raised it to his nose, sniffing.

"Beer? We're to be shellin' lobsterbacks tomorrow and yer fillin' yer belly with beer?" he asked, as if there were no greater sin.

Elijah snatched back his tankard and scowled. A tankard of beer was three pence and he had two shillings in his purse that, if he strung his drinks out long enough, should see him through till the morning. There was a slightly tarnished pound hidden in the front of his left boot just in case Matthew—Mister Cutter—*Matthew*, wished for something a bit dearer than day-old beer.

Of course, he also had a fist full of Continental Bills, but he might as well blow his nose with those for all their use.

By now the barkeep had returned and stood in front of Billy, both hands resting on the bar. Billy kept grinning and leaned forward, one elbow set companionably between them.

"There you are, Thomas! Give us a glass of whiskey and don't be stingy with the pour."

Thomas lifted and eyebrow. "And how are you to be paying for your whiskey, if you don't mind me asking?" The tone in which the question was asked was harmless enough, but everyone knew that the man asking it was far from.

Billy looked shocked, an expression on his face that appeared quite often, usually just before someone else's fist plowed into it. Which, judging by the nasty cut and swelling around his left eye, had already happened at least once that day.

"Why Thomas, we're to be fighting for freedom in jus' a few hours' time and yer worried about the price of a glass of whiskey?"

Elijah took a small sip of his beer.

Thomas straightened and folded his arms across his chest and came as close to appearing like a human piece of granite as anyone possibly could have. "It's not the glass that I worry about with you, Billy. It's the barrel."

Elijah snorted into his beer and tried to cover it with a cough when Billy's gaze cut over to him. Scowling, Billy dropped down onto the stool beside him and threw one hand dismissively into the air.

"All right then, fine. Bring me a pint," he responded. Thomas nodded and reached for a fresh cup. He paused before headed back to the barrel.

"And none of those paper bills either, Billy. It's three bits I'm wanting or there's none for you."

Billy's scowl deepened. "Hell, you'll not support the revolution at all then, Thomas? A fine sort you are."

Thomas merely held his gaze and waited until Billy reached into the pocket of his coat and slapped three pennies down on the bar top.

"I'll support the revolution just as soon as it's worth something more than kindling," Thomas answered, continuing to the back to scoop the beer. A moment later he returned with a barely frothing tankard, which he set down in front of Billy. He snatched up the three pennies and moved off to take care of another customer.

"Tosser," Billy muttered, raising the drink to his lips. He took a long pull that ended with a smack of his lips, and then he leaned back and looked about the room.

Elijah took another sip of his own drink. "So," he began, setting the cup down on the bar. "What matter did you get mixed up in this time?"

Billy did not appear to be listening. His eyes narrowed, and he sat forward on the stool, leaning over toward Elijah. "What? Oh, this." He motioned up to his eye and shook his head. "Don't matter. More importantly, look at that group of four in the back there—no, don't look now. Hold on. All right. Now. See 'em? Bloody loyalists. I spotted 'em as soon as I came in."

Elijah very pointedly *did not* look. "We'll be on the field with the red coats soon enough, Billy. Can't you just wait until then to stir up trouble?"

"Bah. If that Hammiton bloke down in New York had waited, he never would have made off with them cannons, would he?" Billy retorted.

"First off, *Hamilton* didn't steal those cannons by himself. And secondly, I hardly think that the poor souls unfortunate enough to have grabbed your attention have any cannons hidden about their persons."

"Ah, but they might know where they're bein' kept. And if we were to bring that information to Sergeant Whitt he might—"

"—take the credit and leave us to cleaning out the latrines?" Elijah finished for him.

Billy scowled. "All right, fine. Not Sergeant Whitt but one of the others. We could be promoted. You might even be given a command."

It was Elijah's turn to frown into his beer. "They wouldn't give me a command," he disputed darkly. Billy sat back on his stool and held his arms out.

"And why not? You've been to school; yer almost a gentleman."

"Almost," Elijah muttered, bringing his tankard to his lips. His curiosity got the better of him and as he drank, he slid his eyes in the direction that Billy had noted. It was easy enough to see the table that had grabbed Billy's attention. Four men sat at a table with five chairs, each man dressed in rich attire.

He was about to remark to Billy that fine clothing did not automatically equate an undying loyalty to the English Crown when his attention was drawn a few feet to the right, where the second entrance door to the tavern was opening. Elijah found himself straightening on his stool even before he recognized the form of Matthew stepping through the doorway, his hopefully fully buttoned coat folded over one arm. Matthew's own coat was the same dark green as his waistcoat. The tailor paused, his eyes clearly searching the room.

"I'm going to step closer to 'em and see if I can hear anythin'."

Elijah was vaguely aware of Billy speaking and then getting up from his stool. "Right, of course," he replied absently, lifting one hand slightly just as Matthew's gaze landed on him. A smile stretched across the tailor's face, and Elijah felt his own lips lift as he watched the tailor make his way across the room.

"You came!" Elijah exclaimed as soon as Matthew had reached him. The two words came out far more enthusiastic than he had intended. He coughed lightly and felt a flush climbing up the back of his neck. "I mean, so soon. I—that is, I expected it to take a bit longer," he fumbled.

If Matthew thought the exchange strange, he hid it well. Instead, he shrugged slightly and said, "I suppose time flies when one is in need of a button."

Elijah smiled but said nothing. Matthew looked at him. He looked back. The silence between them stretched.

And stretched.

"Well!" Matthew declared, suddenly appearing flustered. He held out the coat on his arm. "Your coat. I'm afraid the button isn't exactly the same but it is quite close."

The tailor's flustering gave Elijah a sense of relief. It was nice to see that he was not the only one so affected. He took the offered coat, lifting the sleeve so that he could inspect the cuff. Sure enough the fourth button did not precisely match the other three—the stamp on it was a bit more decorative—but the size and sheen were nearly spot on. He did not think that Sergeant Whitt was likely to notice the difference.

He nodded and smiled at the tailor. "It is excellent, thank you." And then, without giving himself the chance to back out, he voiced the question he had been practicing in his head all afternoon. "And would you care to join me for a drink? That is, if your other business can wait? It's the least I can do considering your efforts on my behalf."

Elijah was most proud of himself for being able to make it through the short speech without stumbling or adding, *also, you're quite striking and I would like to keep looking at you for as long as you will allow me.*

Matthew's eyebrows lifted, and his mouth dropped open slightly. His eyes flicked away. For a moment, Elijah panicked, wondering if he had been too forward or if perhaps he *had* said that last bit out loud. And then Matthew's gaze met his once more, and he sat down on the stool beside him.

"That would be nice, thank you."

Matthew had barely received a tankard from Thomas (the same, slightly outdated ale that was in Elijah's cup) and few, nonessential questions had been answered (he had just finished his apprenticeship, yes, the condition of Marlborough street was appalling, the weather was quite nice the past few days) when Elijah became suddenly aware of Billy signaling him from across the room. Fortunately Matthew was facing Elijah and so not privy to the exaggerated motions the other young man was making. Elijah realized that if he wanted that to continue to be the case—and he most definitely did—he would have to find out what Billy wanted. Without, god willing, allowing any contact or conversation to ever occur between the two men.

When he saw Billy take a step in the direction of the bar, he knew he had to act immediately. He all but leapt up from his stool, nearly upending his tankard. Luckily Matthew reached out just in time to keep the sturdy mug from tipping over. Elijah felt his ears burn but couldn't waste a moment on embarrassment.

"I, I need to—outside . . . the privy!" he blurted out. He just barely resisted squeezing his eyes shut and added, "I'll be right back," before he ducked away, unable to decipher the look that had been spreading across the tailor's face.

What's to decipher? You're a bumbling idiot who only occasionally manages to squeak out complete, non-mortifying sentences. Clearly he thinks you're an idiot. If he doesn't think you're an idiot, then he probably thinks you're deranged. If he doesn't think—

"Okay, the picture has been painted," he muttered to himself, slipping past the other patrons of the bar. Once he reached Billy, he grabbed hold of the other man's shoulder and propelled them both in the direction of the tavern's back entrance. He kept going until the cool air of the night hit him in the face and the door swung shut behind them. Then he let out a long, heavy sigh that did nothing to ease the tightness in his chest.

"Well what's the matter with you then?" Billy asked, rubbing at the top of his arm where Elijah's grip had squeezed a bit too tightly. Elijah blew out a second long breath and shook his head.

"Absolutely nothing. Now, what was it that you were waving so frantically to me about?"

Billy narrowed his eyes and looked for a moment like he was not at all satisfied with Elijah's answer. Then he abruptly shrugged and rubbed his hands together with a gleefulness that was unsettling.

"Right. Well, those four gits in there left their table and went up to the second floor where the private rooms are. There's a window in the upper hall that I'm sure I can nip through."

Elijah rubbed a hand over his forehead. "Why would you want to do that?" he asked.

Billy folded his arms across his chest. "Are you daft? So I can listen at the door, obviously."

I've only had one and a half pints. That's not nearly enough alcohol to deal with this, Elijah thought. He tipped his head back. Sure enough there was a small, square window about ten to twelve feet overheard. It was even open halfway, to let in the sweet evening breeze, no doubt. But, by Elijah's estimation, Billy was about six feet too short to reach it.

"And how were you planning on getting up there?" he wondered, squinting slightly. He had only a moment to regret the question before Billy's hands came down on his shoulders in one of his hearty pats.

"I jus' need a bit of a boost, that's all. Won't take no time at all." Elijah had a fair idea of what would happen if he tried to refuse and, in the interest of returning to the tavern and hopefully salvaging his current meeting with Master Cutter, he bent one knee and cupped his hands together.

The 'boost' as it were turned into more of a "Let me stand on yer shoulders", and when Elijah re-entered the tavern ten minutes later, he smoothed his hands over his long blonde hair and tightened the tail in the back. There was a dull ache in his shoulders—Christ, Billy had put on a stone or two—but he pulled them back as he stepped to the bar. To his relief, Matthew was still seated on his stool. The tailor gave a smile at his approach that quickly shifted into a frown.

"There appears to be something on your shirt?" he stated once Elijah was within earshot, motioning with one finger.

Elijah looked down and saw the dirt print of one of Billy's boots clearly on display. He had a feeling there was another one somewhere in the center of his back. Lifting a hand to his shoulder, he quickly brushed it away.

"Oh, it's nothing. Just a bit of soot I suppose. The—ah, scullery maid was tossing ashes," he improvised, feeling as if there were a crier standing directly behind him shouting, *Hear ye, hear ye, this lad is a lying toad.*

But Matthew only nodded as if it were the most plausible explanation ever and his smile returned. "I took the liberty of having Thomas top off your cup," he announced, though the moment the words left his mouth, his face pinched in slightly. "I hope that was all right?" he added with uncertainty.

Elijah nodded fiercely and scooped up his tankard, prepared to down the entire contents if only to prove his gratitude. Then the thought occurred to him that that might be a bit odd. He took a sip instead. "Yes, thank you. That's quite kind of you," he managed to get out.

Matthew beamed. "Well, I have the feeling that we are becoming fast friends, are we not?"

Elijah looked down into his cup and felt his ears burn. He swallowed and raised his eyes back to the tailor's—he was certain that he'd never looked into Billy's gaze and experienced the same sort of tumble of feelings as he currently was. Returning Matthew's smile with one of his own, he lifted his tankard.

"To new friendship then."

Matthew lifted his own cup and gamely knocked it lightly against Elijah's. For a moment, Elijah half expected fireworks to explode at the meeting of metal. But there was only a quiet ring that went no further than the space of their conversation.

"To friendship."

Elijah took another pull of beer and searched for something to fill the sudden silence that had fallen between them. They'd already spoken of the weather. Of town. Of Matthew's occupation. He had no desire really to speak of the Revolution, preferring to keep it and the looming battle as far from his mind as possible. Billy had more than enough zeal for the war for the both of them, and Elijah rather hoped to keep this new burgeoning association free of such unpleasant thoughts. He hoped that Matthew might offer something in the manner of a topic but the tailor was still occupied with drinking, his eyes flicking back and forth between Elijah and somewhere over Elijah's right shoulder.

Elijah cleared his throat. "How long have you—"

Matthew began at the same time, "Forgive me but I—"

They stopped, stared and then gave nearly an identical brief chuckle. Elijah motioned with his hand that Matthew should go first. The tailor lowered his head and briefly fidgeted with his pint.

"Pray forgive me, but there's an acquaintance of mine that I just spied that I really must call upon. It would only take a few minutes. I fear if I do not then I will not hear the end of it," he explained, glancing up and giving a small grin.

There were several emotions that flowed through Elijah in the span those three sentences. Sadness that their meeting would be interrupted (*again*), irritation that there was someone else pulling Matthew's attention, a pleasant pinch of delight that the interruption was merely duty and finally, a warm little glow that Matthew had clear intentions of returning.

And so Elijah nodded, striving to appear both calm and composed. "Of course, of course," he declared, settling onto his stool in an attempt to show he had no intention of leaving any time soon. Dawn, and by extension the war, was still quite a ways off.

Matthew stood quickly, set his tankard down on the bar and turned to make way toward the back of the tavern. Elijah followed him with his eyes curious as to who it was he was meeting. The tailor easily made his way through the crowd, not pausing to greet or speak with any of the patrons he passed.

"Elijah."

Elijah turned at the sound of Thomas' voice. The bartender stood in front of him on the other side of the bar, his face drawn tight in a mixture of resignation and indignation. Elijah was fairly certain he was current with his tab so he felt comfortable that he was not the source of the man's irritation. That, of course, only left one other option.

"Yes, Thomas?" he asked, hoping he was mistaken.

"Would you care to explain to me why Billy Boyle is currently dangling from one of my second-story windows?"

Elijah winced. "Is he?" he asked, with an ignorance not entirely feigned. After all, Billy had been climbing *through* the window last time he had seen him.

Thomas laid a hand on the bar top, his fingers tapping a slow, steady rhythm. "Aye, he is. Damn near scared the life out of the serving girl up there."

Elijah rubbed a hand over the back of his neck. "Look, I honestly don't—"

Thomas lifted both his hands, cutting him off. "I don't rightly care what he was doing. Just do me a favor; go get him down and tell him that he'll have to find his spirits somewhere else this evening. I'll not serve him another drop."

Nodding, Elijah swiftly straightened off his stool. He chanced a look at Thomas' face and saw the vein in his forehead thrum, a sure sign of the temper currently held in check. It was a risk to ask but he absolutely *had* to know.

"Does that—I mean—am I—"

"Are you currently hanging out one of my windows?" Thomas interrupted, his heavy brows drawing together.

Elijah silently shook his head.

"Then you can stay and finish your parley." Before Elijah could think to ask him what he meant by that, Thomas jerked a thumb towards the tavern exit. Elijah took the gesture for what it meant and pushed his way across the room.

He was just pushing through the door when he heard the *thud*, followed by a "fuck me" and a sickly *crunch*. Just a few feet away Billy lay crumpled on the ground, groaning and clutching at his left boot. With a sigh, Elijah stepped over to him, crouching down. It took Billy a second to realize he was there.

"Oh, Elijah, thank the lord. I think I've broken my fucking foot. Help me up."

Elijah did not move. "Did the Tories have anything of import to say?" he asked instead.

"Bugger the Tories! Can't you see I'm in pain? I need a nip of whiskey to dull it. Be a kind soul Elijah and help me inside."

"Thomas has thrown you out for the evening. You terrified one of the serving ladies."

"Ah, bugger it. Well. I suppose we ought to head back to camp then. One of the lads'll have a bottle of something to pass the rest of the evening."

For a brief—but not *that* brief—moment, Elijah considered standing up and walking away, leaving Billy to sit in the cold and painful consequences of his behavior. For once. But as satisfying as such a decision might feel it was also thoughtless and unbecoming.

He stood up. "Wait here," he instructed tersely, because unbecoming or not, he was still annoyed to have his evening cut short.

Billy scowled up at him. "Where the hell are you goin'?" he demanded.

Elijah didn't bother to answer. He stepped back toward the door and just barely resisted shoving it open, though he did push with perhaps a bit more force than necessary. So intent was he on returning to the bar so that he could leave his regrets with Matthew that he did not notice the tailor in front of him until he had nearly bowled him over.

"Oh! I'm terribly sorry," he apologized, catching hold of Matthew's arm to steady him. Matthew waved the apology away with one hand, brushing the other over the front of his vest.

"It's fine. But are you all right? You look a bit out of sorts," he observed.

Elijah frowned and released his arm. Not knowing what else to do with them, he tucked his hands into the pockets of his trousers.

"I'm afraid my evening is at its end. A friend of mine has done minor injury to himself and requires assistance in getting home."

"Oh, I'm sorry to hear that! Nothing serious I hope?"

Nothing a few knocks about the head won't cure, Elijah thought. Out loud, he replied, "Just a turn of the ankle I believe."

"Ah, well I'll hope for a speedy recovery for your friend. I, too, must say goodnight. I have another . . . matter to see to."

Elijah nodded—he had been aware that the evening had come with a pre-determined ending, even without Billy's antics to help it along. Now that the end had arrived, though, he couldn't help but feel disappointed with its timing. He took some comfort in the fact that Matthew appeared just as reluctant to say farewell.

"Of course," he said, trying to work out in his head how best to ask for another meeting, perhaps somewhere Billy Boyle was far less likely to patronize. Each offer and phrase that came to his head seemed too obvious, too bothersome or too foolish.

He supposed he could always just tear another button off his jacket.

"You may find me in the shop most days of the week," Matthew was saying. The tailor smiled and tilted his head slightly. "I hope that you will feel free to call upon me again. Even if you have no cloth that needs mending," he added with a slight cough.

Elijah felt his chest expand and wondered if anyone else in the room could see his heart as it attempted to beat its way out of his breast. He could feel that he was grinning a bit more broadly than was natural but couldn't quite bring his cheeks under control.

"I would be delighted," he heard himself say. And then, deciding it was probably best to make an exit before the giddiness bubbling up inside of him made its way out of his mouth, he held out his hand.

Matthew clasped it firmly and then leaned forward, placing a quick kiss on first his right cheek and then his left.

"Until we meet again then!" he proclaimed and then, he was gone.

Elijah stood still for a moment then raised a hand to one cheek, as if he could feel the goodbye gesture imprinted on his skin. A bit dazed, he drifted back to the bar and picked up his coat from where he had placed it earlier. Folding it over one arm, he coasted out of the tavern and onto the street. He found his eyes drawn upwards to where the stars glittered and sparkled. Had he ever noticed before how beautiful the sky looked at night?

He had gone nearly two blocks before he stopped, turned around and went back to get Billy.

When dawn broke, so did battle.

Any stars that might have been lingering in the sky were quickly hidden behind clouds of grey smoke from fired rifles. The sun rose but spirits fell, and each *crack* of gunfire sent men to their knees, their backs, or their rest.

Elijah's hands trembled as he poured powder into the barrel of his gun; his fingers felt icy and stiff even as sweat gathered at his brow and under the heavy weight of his coat. He dropped in a bullet and tapped it down with the ramrod. His shoulders jerked as he heard the cacophony of shouted orders, painful screams and explosions. The smoke stung his eyes and the taste of ash burned in the back of his mouth. No amount of swallowing could budge the lump that seemed fixed in his throat.

There came the light touch of a breeze upon his face, and the fog of war parted. Out of the corner of his eye he saw a flash of red and raised his musket to his shoulder to fire. He heard the wet thump a second before the pain burst open in his chest. As he fell to his knees, he wedged the butt of his musket into the ground and caught himself. His breath came and went in short, sharp gasps that did nothing to fill his lungs.

Blinking, he raised his head, just enough to see through the window that had delivered death.

Not more than twenty yards away, his red coat bright under the sun, Matthew Cutter stood, his rifle slowly lowering, a look of horror stretched across his handsome face.

For reasons that Elijah could not comprehend, as the life drained out of him, his eyes focused on Matthew's right arm, which held steady the stock of the rifle. In particular, he stared at the navy and white stripes on the cuff of the tailor-turned-soldier's coat.

He was missing a button.

"Hold on. This one don't look too bad."

"Don't look bad? He caught it right in the chest!"

"Yeah, but see there? Not much damage elsewhere. Here, give me a hand."

Elijah opened his eyes, and it was no longer day. He saw the bright glow of lanterns and, just beyond that, the twinkle of the stars. The smoke was gone, as was the sound of men being broken and beaten. The pain in his chest was gone, too.

He sat up and looked around. Surrounding him was the debris of battle; bodies lay crumpled in ways that suggested hope had long since flown from the box. Nearby was a cart, half-filled with more bodies, and two men who were headed directly toward him.

Alarmed, he scrambled to his feet. "What do you want?" he shouted, throwing his hands out in front of him. Neither man responded. Elijah noticed something immediately.

He had gotten to his feet.

His body had not.

He looked at his hands and saw that they were as insubstantial as mist; he brought them together and they passed through each other like water.

The two men lifted his body up; one held him upright while the other briskly pulled his coat off. Once it was free, the one holding him let his body drop unceremoniously to the ground. The one that held his coat gave it a quick shake and held it up.

"See? Practically new. Hardly any blood on it at all. Tell you what; we got a fresh batch of recruits that will be needing one of these."

"Boots look new, too. Might as well take them. He ain't going to be needing them."

Elijah stared as the men stripped his body of what they saw as useful before they tossed it up onto the cart and moved onto the next. As they began to move away, he felt a tug that pulled him towards them. He walked, or drifted, closer.

They'd thrown his coat onto a pile on the front seat of the wagon, just behind the horses. There was a small glow in the darkness, near the bottom of the sleeve. He placed his hand over it and felt something like warmth pulsing from it.

He sighed. "Well, so much for revolution."

Alternate Ending

Nicole DeGennaro

Don't look yet!" she said, laughing.

I let out an exaggerated sigh as I kept my back to her. The fur on my arms stood on end as she worked a new spell; a moment later the faint scent of something burning wafted toward me, indicating a successful bit of magic.

I still find the odor hard to describe: not quite that of singed fur or leaves, not quite sulfuric or pleasant. The closest I've settled on is sour perfume—a great quantity of decaying flowers tossed on a fire.

"Okay, turn around," my sister said, and I spun toward her. I expected her to be holding something, a small figment pulled from her imagination and brought to brief, beautiful life. Instead she had turned away from me, her wings spread wide to accentuate a perfect rainbow arcing against the flawless lavender sky.

"Nice," I said. Not a unique spell, but advanced for her age.

"Shhhh," she scolded me, as if she could sense the slight disappointment in my voice. I had become so used to the wonders of magic that to be impressed, I needed more than my little sister creating something out of nothing.

But of course she outdid herself. As I watched, the rainbow began to drip, falling as a multicolored rain around us from the cloudless sky. Where the drops hit the ground, flowers bloomed.

I had never seen anything like it. I haven't seen anything like it since.

We were capable of anything, but when the time came we chose to do nothing.

If we had had some sign of our coming fate, would that have changed anything? When something is ubiquitous, what would it take to convince you to give it up? My world engaged in a willful ignorance—sacrificing anything for power over the fabric of the universe. The greatest magic my people ever performed was the illusion of control we cast over ourselves.

My generation would be the last to use magic on my world, although we were not the first by a long shot. I'm not sure I would have given up my power if I had known the perils in advance. Our lives revolved around its use; its discovery had irreversibly altered our society long before my time. Magic became a birthright; we had no choice but to use it. And we took great joy in the using, because we did not realize what we would lose.

I'm not sure where Vlanna is; I am stuck on a strange world, and I can only hope that she too escaped and is stuck elsewhere, safe. Or maybe she found another solution. She often made the choice I wouldn't, but in this instance I pray she chose safety over courage.

After all this time, I've had to assume my world perished. Otherwise, my exile is a punishment instead of a reward. Otherwise I am a coward.

"Hey, Shurra?" my sister said, climbing into my cushioned nest next to me. Her delicate hands fidgeted; her wings fluttered.

"What's the matter?" I put down the puzzle sphere I had been toying with, an object meant to be solved using magic. But I hadn't been able to work the spell to move the pieces.

She shrugged but chewed her lip. After a moment, she reached for the sphere. I had seen her solve it before, but I gave it to her anyway—thinking she wanted to occupy her hands while she talked about her worries.

Instead she worked a spell, the one to activate the pieces. I couldn't follow the finer movements of her fingers or understand the more complicated words she muttered, but when she finished the sour perfume filled the air around us, more pungent than ever. We coughed, waiting for it to dissipate, for the pieces of the sphere to shift. My sister kept her gaze locked on mine, expectation all over her face. As the odor lingered, longer than it used to, as the pieces of the sphere remained stationary, she waited for me to give a voice to her fear.

My hearts pounded at a roaring pace as I waited, waited. I would have waited forever rather than admit what the inactive puzzle meant. But she put the sphere down and took my cold hands in her warm ones. Her wide, dark eyes mirrored my concern as the smell finally faded.

She opened her mouth, but I interrupted. I didn't want to hear her say what I wouldn't.

"That spell is difficult," I said, and her face fell. She looked away from me. "Everyone fails a spell sometimes." The words brought me a desperately sought relief.

"I did it correctly," she said in a soft voice as she climbed out of the nest. I reached for her but stopped short of making contact. She sighed, then faced me again just as my hand fell back to my lap. "When did you last do a successful spell?"

The question was half challenge, half gentle urging. The disappointment on her face stung like a wound; I wanted to erase it. I tried to remember—but unlike her, I failed spells daily. So I hadn't taken note even when a few easier ones sputtered out—even when my technique had been flawless.

I couldn't recall my last successful act of magic, but I couldn't admit that ignorance. I used so many spells in a day that they ran together, mundane as the weather: only noticeable when somehow exceptional.

"I think...yesterday?" I can't explain why I lied, why I thought she wouldn't catch it.

She nodded once, a deep frown of disbelief shaping her face. "Never mind, then."

The disappointment I sparked in her that day never fully dissipated. I so easily bought into my own falsehoods, ensconced in their comfort, that I wished for her to join me. But she wouldn't, and I wouldn't face the truth.

When I look back, I try to do so with an honesty I lacked at the time. If my sister is trapped elsewhere, I hope she can sense this, my effort to face the worst of myself. I'm trying to live up to who she believed I could be.

I am not ignorant to the fact that it might be too late for that. At the very least, I will not allow myself to indulge in lies again. It is a slow, painful process. Bridging the gap between my natural inclinations and who my sister wanted me to be is proving a challenge. Each time I go over the memories, I uncover a new facet, a deeper layer of my flaws. Perhaps this excavation will be endless; perhaps I am made of nothing but mistakes.

I am alive—so does that make my choices wrong at all? If survival is the ultimate imperative, I have succeeded. Although I am stuck on a different world, in a strange form, powerless. Any others of us that escaped would be in a similar position, I imagine. If we are all stuck in new forms, does that count as survival? Whoever remains is the last of our kind wherever we have landed, and we would not recognize one another if we were face to face.

In some ways the truth is as complicated as anything else. Perhaps that is why my sister could never put it into words, either. She didn't try to replace it with something else, but many times she did not speak frankly when she could have. If she had forced me from my comfort, perhaps things would be different.

This slow excavation has revealed to me a chasm between deciding to act and performing an action, and it is one I have yet to traverse. The distance and depth freezes me in place; it is easier to follow my old patterns. I have had numerous opportunities already on this new world to be the version of me that Vlanna hoped for, but I have yet to make that leap. Next time, I tell myself. Always next time. Even though at some point there will be a last time. That knowledge has not yet been enough to push me to action.

"There's an image of the creature," Vlanna said, breathless, right before the end. The sour perfume filled every space, as if fields of dying flowers perpetually burned around us.

I had already seen. The topic had taken over every conversation; some people even conjured the image when words failed, although the magic didn't last long if it succeeded at all. The creature had come after weeks of odd objects appearing at random, sometimes crushing clusters of nests. Items we had never seen, could not imagine, made of unnatural materials. But the creature was the first living form to appear.

Jagged and dark as a void, crawling around on two or four legs as it pleased. It came out of nothingness, and its first attack sent an entire colony into oblivion. It had erased two more nest clusters before anyone had survived long enough to pass on an image.

"Someone's magic probably got out of hand," I said, eager to deny that we did indeed face the end. Plenty of magical mistakes had happened before as we all tried to outperform each other. But no one had managed to cast more than a simple conjuring for weeks. Even if they had, the creature did not resemble the consequences of a misfiring spell. Instead of hinting at the presence of malevolent magic, it suggested the absence of everything.

I would like to claim I recognized my statement as a lie when I said it, but I can't ascribe that much credit to my past self. So I shrugged my sister off. Vlanna shot me a harsh scowl, and I averted my eyes. She perched next to me, ducking until I had to look at her.

"They're going to reactivate the alert network," she said, her gaze daring me to try and explain that away.

"Who even owns a working receiver anymore?" I scoffed. Technological development had ground to a halt with the widespread use of magic. It fulfilled every need, took up no space, and cost nothing. It freed us, we thought. It would last forever, we believed.

My sister shook her head, opened her mouth and closed it again. I wonder if she had meant to finally drag me from my denial. Why did she decide against it?

I ignored the signs as I had been taught, tried to avoid the insurmountable. But I've since learned that it is always, always better to try and find a way around, across, or through.

The same creatures threaten my new home, and I am trying to keep this world's denizens from repeating my mistakes. In the process, maybe I won't repeat them either. It is easier in some ways—not many here can perform magic. It is also harder—somehow, the voids have already begun infiltrating. Even if I wanted to take action, I can no longer cast spells. I had to pay for my successful escape with my power. I had no idea that would be the cost when I made my choice. I'm not sure that knowledge would have changed my decision.

But I have found—or been found by—one who can do magic. In some ways she reminds me of Vlanna. I wish I could help her, but she thinks of me as a pet, leaves me at her home when she goes to defend her world. In this way she is already better than me, not in skill but in strength of character. With fragments of spells and techniques that my people deemed fit only for children, she uses her abilities to fight the voids.

There is danger in that, too. Magic doesn't recognize intentions—it uses the same ingredients regardless. And a key component in any spell is the same compound that composes the barriers between the worlds.

I've been lying to myself still. The excuses come so easily even as I try to excise them. It is true my companion treats me as a pet, yet if I insisted on following her, she would let me. I never insist.

Even though I am more honest with myself about my memories from my world, I have allowed some falsehoods to linger. My people did have a sign of our fate, of what would come. We had been trained to accept it, and I never questioned that training. But the sour perfume pervades all of my memories, so noticeable upon looking back that I can't explain how we ever feigned ignorance.

Nothing visible had ever been burning, so we assumed the odor meant nothing. By the time Vlanna and I began using magic, our people had been doing so for centuries. If the smell had had no obvious consequence at that point, we reasoned, it never would.

What a simple trap we set for ourselves.

When a bit of the barrier between worlds is singed away, it creates that bitter scent. Each spell cast, whether with good or ill intent, singes a small hole in the veil between worlds.

By manipulating the fabric of the universe, we destroy it.

I think my old world is the reason the voids can already access my new one. By the time my people realized the source of the stench, we had ruined too much of the barrier to repair what we had done. In the end, my old world was not annihilated but assimilated. Other worlds burst through, flooded into ours.

If any remnant of my home world still exists between the others, it would be a borderland of sorts. The remains might have facilitated the voids' invasion of this world. Or perhaps they followed me here; I can't be certain.

The thin areas of the veil around this world can be repaired—the voids can be locked out. There is plenty of fabric here for that. But only if these beings realize it in time.

I keep hoping that revisiting my memories will give me the push I need to cross the chasm, to help somehow. I have not yet tested the physical capabilities of my new form. But I will remain inert until I shed everything but the truth, until I stop using my recollections as one final escape from reality.

My world perished, and that fact makes me no less a coward.

I did see Vlanna's rainbow magic one more time.

And I know what happened to her.

"No!" my sister said, resisting as I grabbed her.

"Come on!" I took her hand, on the last day. When the magic had run out and the voids had come. The sour perfume had been overwhelmed by smoke carrying the stench of scorched fur and flesh, demolished lives. The sun hung high and red, obscured by ash. But along the horizon, all color and carnage disappeared into eternal absence. The inky dark took the ground, the trees, the strange objects.

I pulled my sister after me. With the barrier around our world destroyed, we could push through those that surrounded other places. I had seen some of our people do so to escape. So I led my sister toward the closest foreign object, hoping it indicated an access point, hoping we would be able to seal the way behind us.

"NO!" she yelled again, resisting my pull. Our hands separated.

I turned around then, hoping to take hold of her again. That might have been another mistake, the last in a long line. Maybe I should have kept going, pretended I didn't feel her hand release from mine. She stood still as the world fell apart, posing a silent challenge to me in the jut of her chin.

"We can fight," she said. "We should fight."

"There's no magic left!"

I reached out as the darkness snaked toward her. She took a step away from me and broke my heart. I wish the voids had taken me then.

Instead, somehow, Vlanna performed a spell. She must have pulled the necessary ingredient from another world's barrier or from the voids themselves. But at the time it went beyond magic—it was a miracle. A rainbow burst to vibrant life against the chaos, too bright, almost blinding. The voids recoiled—one vaporized. The rainbow exploded into a hail of light, cutting streaks through the nothingness to reveal our world still intact beneath. It hadn't been destroyed yet, just obscured. Mid-consumption.

I should have joined her. We might have succeeded.

But the light faded; the voids regrouped. My sister prepared another spell, her wings spread and beating to lift her off the ground as the darkness advanced. She fought like a child, with the tactics of an optimist. A rainbow—an attack of hope, to use light in the way she did. It might have worked if I had been able to find that hope in myself.

Instead, I turned away. I left her there.

I would like to blame something else for my choices and mistakes, to say my society raised me to believe that I had no choice and because of that could make no mistake. But my struggle to accept ownership of my actions makes them no less my own. After all, the same society raised my sister, and she never shied away from acknowledging the truth.

Sometimes I even try to blame Vlanna. I want to believe she never tried to force me from the solace of my lies, but all her actions say otherwise. She attempted; I refused.

I'm not sure who is in a better place. I survived, but now I have to live with myself. Without her.

There are so many things we turn away from, and so few we turn around for. One is so much easier even though both are essentially the same action. At the end, my sister and I made the same choice with different intent. We both turned—her toward, me away. The distinction is minor, a matter of perspective, yet no detail is more important.

But the universe does not care about intention and perspective. So many actions have the same consequence regardless of the impetus. Perhaps intention is a construct we use to clear our conscience. If our action is detrimental, we can soothe ourselves by saying we meant no harm. Maybe the idea of intent is nothing more than a comforting lie. My people did not intend to destroy our world—but we did. I didn't intend to be a coward—but I was. Am.

This is how I circle back around to inaction. This is the loop in which I am stuck. I have not yet found my way around, across, or through.

But I am not turning away.

Part IV

Knowledge

1. The theoretical or practical understanding of a subject.

2. Awareness or familiarity gained by experience of a fact or situation.

Temple Break

Lara Eckener

We grow trellised around songs
dedicated to our skin. Know the words
well, know them alone in the dark.
Know them as lies that need to be outrun.

Withdrawing, we stack our modern hymnals,
so the spines lodge a broken complaint,
and go to find sanctuary somewhere else,
anywhere, some place bright and godless.

It's hard to feel haunted where it's never dark.
When the old music beckons we drown it out
with new hymns, fumbling for the words with
enough power to be stitched into our skin.

We were not knit together to be
left alone. We do not know who we are,
but we are not the girls they first presented
to the darkness between the stars.

Frustrated and too full of knowing we
sweep glasses out of bare cabinets,
break plates and shake the rugs out
onto the floor, trace galaxies in the dust.

Temple Break

We ask, how could the stars hold sway
over us, when during the course of a life
a woman will shed a universe's worth
of her own dust without even trying?

We've absorbed the glittering never-dark
from the city streets. It's shooting
through our cracks. Now we can see
what the old songs meant by glow.

They meant that one day we will burn
with a knowledge of ourselves. Above,
the stars will shudder. We will understand those
trellis songs were not metaphors, but promises:

Take no gods over yourself, you are
the envy of the stars. He will welcome
you in their light but, you do not need them.
You are what they'll become. You already glow.

A Quiet Anger

Christine Ricketts

Near the edge of the town is a park.

It's a nice enough park, with soft green grass that tickles your ankles and a couple of tall shady trees to sit or play beneath.

In the center, there is a cluster of wooden benches, the perfect place to sit and enjoy a sunny morning or fading twilight.

After dinner, when the sun is working its way down toward the horizon, the park is almost always full. Kids running, chasing, kicking all sorts of different colored spheres or ducking in, around and up into those ever-inviting trees. Adults gather around the benches, chatting with each other while the kids burn through their nearly inexhaustible stores of energy.

In the morning there are a few joggers that cut across the grass as they seek the mindless rhythm of motion. Dogs are walked, sniffing along invisible ley lines and carving up territories like warring nations.

But later, in the afternoon, halfway through the clock's infinite cycle, the park is empty. Always. Deliberately empty. If asked, no one in the surrounding neighborhood would agree—while they don't ever go in the afternoon, too busy, too something to bother, surely somebody does. Kids on weekends or days off from school or adults at home who need a break from their houses, a turn in the fresh air.

They're certain, convinced and completely wrong.

No one goes to the park in the afternoon.

Until someone does. It's just after twelve o'clock on a day like any other. The sun is directly overhead, shining brightly down over the small circle of benches. He is out for a walk away from the confines of the work that he enjoys but needs a moment or two away from. The neighborhood is new to him, he only moved in a few days ago, but he remembers the

153

park from his first visits of interest. He doesn't have a dog or a child but he might in the future. Probably the dog because children are still a long way off. But hopefully not too far off—it's early, way too early, but he's got a good feeling that maybe he's falling into the big "L."

But there's time he thinks, time to enjoy the journey and an afternoon stroll before heading back to the desk in his tiny but cozy apartment.

The park is as nice as he remembers, maybe even nicer because he's on foot and not snatching glances out the window of his car as he cruises by, listening to the instructional chirping of his GPS. He plans just to walk around the edges; a complete circuit might take him twenty minutes if he goes slow.

He's only taken a couple of steps when his plans change. There's something blindingly bright over near the benches, like sunshine glaring off a mirror. It draws his eyes and then his feet as his curiosity runs off ahead of him. For half a moment he thinks that maybe something is on fire—he can smell the heavy scent of char and soot—but then it's gone and so is the glare.

Seated instead on one of the benches is a young woman with very fair hair. He starts to turn away, not wanting to disturb her, when he hears a quiet sob and sees the glint of tears staining her face. He sits down on one of the benches—not too close. He doesn't want to startle her.

"Miss? Are you all right?" he asks, as gently as he can. He doesn't think that she's noticed him yet, thinks she's too caught up in her troubles.

She doesn't jump like he worried she might. Her head lifts and her face is full of more sadness than seems possible for a face to hold. She doesn't answer his question. He tries again.

"Are you hurt? Can I do anything to help?" There has to be something, anything that will offer some kind of comfort.

She looks at him and he feels his own eyes begin to fill because there is such sorrow in her gaze. And then a sigh escapes her and resignation floods her features.

"He brought me here. Said it was special. That it would always be my special place." Her voice is soft and quiet. He drifts closer, almost without realizing it.

"Did he leave you here? Do you need a ride somewhere?" he asks. His voice sounds loud even in his own ears.

She looks at him and he can see the reflection of the sun burning in her eyes.

"He hurt me. He hurt me because he could. And then they hurt me, too. Because they could. Then they brought me here." Another long, mournful sigh and she adds,

"Now I'll hurt you."

Before the words can register in his mind, her hands shoot out and grip his forearms. He tries to jerk away but her hold is like iron.

It's not a reflection that he sees now—her eyes are burning. Tiny suns that seethe with uncontrolled fire. Where her fingernails dig into his skin burns with the same intolerable heat. Pain and panic twist up inside him and the tears that come into his eyes now are for himself.

"Please. Please don't. I . . I didn't do anything to you," he begs.

She looks at him and there is still sadness and sorrow and resignation in those twin suns.

"I know. But this is what I am. This is what they made me. This is all that's left." She leans in closer, close enough to whisper. There are flames covering her, covering him. He can feel them eating away at his body.

"They're still hurting me. They're hurting you too."

The pain is unbearable and he wants to scream but he can't gather the air into his lungs. She is still looking at him and he tries to plead with his eyes, long past the point where it would matter.

There's a flare of light, like the glare of the sun off the tops of waves in the ocean. And then the benches are empty save for a small mound of white ash that covers one side. The wind blows and, almost like an invisible hand swiping over the worn wood, scatters the ash.

The park is quiet.

The Modern Phoenix

Nicole DeGennaro

When Natalie wakes with a gasping breath, there are a few things she immediately knows:

She is being restrained.

She has undergone some kind of surgery.

She did not consent to whatever has been done to her.

Her mouth is dry in a way it only ever is after an anesthetic, when her mind is forced so far into unconsciousness it forgets to produce saliva. The lingering grogginess that stymies her ability to focus confirms her suspicion: she has been operated on. But she isn't in a hospital—there are no vital sign monitors, no privacy curtain, no constant murmur of activity just outside the door to her room.

She tries to pull up her most recent memory to give her any clue to what has happened. But there isn't much coming through the dissipating fog. Just her usual routine: work, getting a drink with co-workers, heading home. If that was yesterday or last week now, she isn't sure.

Has she been in some kind of accident? She doubts it—her parents and sister would have been notified, but no one is around; no flowers or get well cards, either. Perhaps she has been kidnapped, maybe an organ taken for the black market? Something is different about her body, but she can't pinpoint it. After taking a deep breath, she starts at her feet and works her way up. She's able to move all her extremities against the restraints, doesn't feel a pull on her skin from stitches or staples. She can't lift her head high enough to see the rest of her body; her neck is stiff, and there is some kind of padding keeping her upper body as still as possible. She is physically intact, but she is still certain something is different; it's the subtle disorientation of entering a familiar room that seems unchanged at first glance until you realize all the furniture has been moved a few inches to the left. Her stomach sinks.

An obnoxious electric buzzing fills her head as the grogginess clears. Maybe there is some electronic equipment outside her line of sight, but the noise quickly reaches a fever pitch, setting her hair on end. She hisses and turns her head as much as she can, but she sees no equipment. She is alone in a sterile room.

Her heart skips several beats as she suppresses the thought that hits her. But as soon as it forms, she is certain it's true: The buzzing is coming from her. It's inside her head. She's never experienced a noise like this before. It's more than the ever-present hum of electricity that the human brain has learned to filter out. This sound is reverberating in her bones, rippling through her blood, weaving between the gyri in her brain. It's coming from somewhere inside her and infiltrating every inch, as much a part of her as her nervous system. And it's still somehow getting louder.

"What did they do?" she asks herself, hoping her voice might stop the noise or wake her from what she hopes is a vivid nightmare. Her voice is hoarse and undercut with an electronic quality, as if she had spoken through a popping microphone. That's when the panic hits her, tingling through her extremities before punching her in the gut and closing its fist around her throat.

She doesn't know who "they" are, but it must have been a joint effort to kidnap and operate on her. Definitely a 'they', and at some point they'll return.

As she begins to struggle against the restraints, the buzzing crescendos until she's wincing, almost paralyzed. Then the panic disappears. Not a slow retreat—a real vanishing act. One moment there, making it hard to breathe or think or speak, and the next gone without even one final skip of her heart or short breath.

`Panic is not helpful,` a robotic voice in her head says, replacing the buzzing.

She swallows, her mouth dry again. Her whole body starts to shake as she adds something else to her short list of facts:

She knows what they did to her.

As tears prick the corners of her eyes and a lump forms in her throat, the buzzing returns and overrides the urge.

`Crying is not necessary.`

"Fu—" she starts, but what she wants to say is snatched from her lips.

"F—" she tries again, her face hot from frustration. The invader in her consciousness stops her again. She's been made a prisoner in her own body.

Fuck you, she thinks.

`Cursing is not ladylike.`

"It's a prototype, of course. We've had a hell of a time finding volunteers," says the man in the lab coat.

She has been put on display. She is on a chair in a room by herself. No longer strapped down, but given strict commands to remain seated and as still as possible. The programming won't let her disobey.

That is how she has come to think of the buzzing and the robotic voice. They are part of the same thing—an object that has been implanted within her to override her emotional responses. Once she had heard the voice, she had recalled a conversation from years ago, when a friend and fellow scientist floated an idea for a new technology. She had advised him against pursuing it, and he had not mentioned it again.

She had forgotten about it until she had woken up with it inside her head. And now she sees that same man standing on the other side of the glass, extolling the wonders of his invention to a group of men and women in suits and lab coats. Praising her for her selfless act of volunteering in front of those investors and future users of his technology. They leer and nod, none seeming as repulsed as she had been all those years ago.

She doesn't take her eyes off him, does her best to try and understand why he's done this to her. A small ember of rage burns deep in her, and she tries to communicate it to him without alerting the programming. But he doesn't acknowledge her; there is only a hunger in his eyes, his ego salivating for fame and fortune.

"You say this has military use, which I think is obvious," a woman in a suit says. "But why is the prototype not a soldier or some other type of martial personnel, then?" She looks Natalie up and down, evaluating her like a piece of furniture at a yard sale. *Convince me I need this*, her detached expression says.

"Precisely because I don't think the military applications are a hard sell. But there are certain...domestic applications as well," the man in the lab coat says. She refuses to even think his name because he is in no way the person she befriended. When she can't get through to him, she looks at another man and woman, both in lab coats—his research assistants, people she also considered friends. Maybe one of them will see her distress, will help her somehow.

But one of them refuses to look directly at her, keeping his gaze just to the right or left. The other has the same ego hunger about her and looks at Natalie without seeing her. They too have been rendered useless, chosen by him for the traits that would make them obedient. And for those that don't have traits he can manipulate, he created the contraption he put in her.

The buzzing in her head intensifies, and an alarm goes off in the room, set off by one of the myriad sensors attached to her for his circus act.

"Ah, the device is working right now to override some emotional impulse," he says with a slight sneer.

`Anger is unbecoming,` the robotic voice informs her.

Well it's all I have, she thinks—at least its control doesn't reach that far. Not in the prototype, anyway. Something of herself remains untainted.

And I plan to use it.

The man in the lab coat comes by later, once everyone else has left. No suits, no shtick, just him and her and what he's done. He still wears the lab coat, as if he is trying to convince her of the merits of his device. Or maybe it's meant to taunt her: *I've ended your career, your life, to advance my own.*

Because he's gone beyond forging her consent on some paperwork; he must have lied to her own lab assistants and co-workers, told them she made this decision. They shouldn't have believed him—her work on nanotechnology to treat diseases has little overlap with his research—but there would have been no reason for them to doubt him. Even if they had suspicions, he had the paperwork to back his claim.

Yes, now she's certain that his wearing the lab coat is about dominance, to show he's won a battle that he imagined. There had been no rivalry, no hurt feelings, no career sabotage. But he had perceived something differently—she can't fathom what—and had decided to hobble her, transform her into a subservient cyborg.

The full implications of her situation begin to settle within her, planting a deep unease in her gut as her mind recoils from reality.

He smiles, as if he can see her thoughts and where the last one trailed off. He has stood in silence for minutes taking her in, ogling her with far more interest and intent than the woman in the suit earlier. She tries to speak, yell, curse him out. The buzzing in her head is deafening. The alarm in the room begins to blare.

There is no reason to speak.

"Music to my ears," he says as he motions to the speakers to indicate the alarm. She manages to clench a fist before her hand is forced to uncurl. The lag catches her attention but is gone before she can be sure it was anything. Still, she tucks that moment away, storing it along with the bits of herself she is salvaging from the wreckage he has made of her.

"Things are going to be so much better for us now," he says when the alarm stops, approaching her with the saunter of a cat with all the time in the world to pounce. "We were drifting apart because of your career, but I care about you, about us. I want us to be happy again. I'm sure you understand that."

He has not asked her a question, so the programming is not allowing her to speak. But she would be too shocked to say anything. Not only has this man become unrecognizable, but his description of their relationship is also alien. She can't figure out how he got from a few scientific discussions and after-work drinks with co-workers to what he's done to her and what she fears he plans to do next.

"Now there won't have to be any competition between us," he says. "There won't be any hurt feelings." He is close enough to touch her, and he does so without hesitation. He caresses her cheek with a pasty, clammy hand. When she tries to pull away the buzzing comes, the alarm intensifies. He grins.

Then his hand slides down her neck to her clavicle, where it lingers only for a moment before slipping further and cupping her right breast. He leans over to whisper in her ear, his erection pressing against her thigh. Her brain is in a whirlwind of revulsion and fear spinning so fast the contraption can hardly keep up.

"There won't be anymore 'no's.'" He squeezes her breast, too hard to be about her pleasure. His breath is hot on her skin.

"Say my name." It is a command she doesn't want to obey, and there is a brief moment where she thinks his device is too overwhelmed and has overlooked her mental refusal. But before she can test it by saying something else, it catches up and forces her to acquiesce.

She has to say his name, but she refuses to hear it, to think it. The moan that escapes him, though, she can't ignore. Bile rises in her throat for a fraction of a second before that urge, too, is overridden.

"N—" She attempts to make her nonconsent clear, but she is not permitted to speak even that simple word.

He continues to grope her, and she wants to scream, punch him, spit on him, run away—anything but experience what is happening. *No. No. No*, she thinks, wrapping herself in the word to block out the feeling of him against her. The alarm blares ceaselessly as he rapes her, but no one is around to help.

Afterward, when he is gone and she is alone, the least she would like to do is cry.

`Crying is not necessary`, the voice reminds her.

He only puts her on display in the lab a few more times. After that, he takes her back to his house, claiming it's the next phase of the experiment—seeing how well the prototype operates in the real world. But it has been hard for her to judge the passage of time in a room with no windows or clocks, so she is not sure exactly how long it has been since she first awoke with his device in her.

The sunlight dazzles her when he leads her out of the lab to his car. As she squints and blinks back tears, he speaks.

"You've adjusted to the emotion override faster than I thought; I expected it to take two weeks at least."

From that, she assumes she has been in his lab a week or less. The programming forces her to get into the passenger seat of his car at his command, but she does not resist, so there is no terrible buzzing. She has cultivated an inner calm that she pours her energy into maintaining to save her the constant trauma of the noise. But her curiosity has been piqued by his statement.

It takes her the first ten minutes of the car ride to figure out what he means. It is only as she cautiously begins to examine the time since her alteration, tiptoeing around any related emotions, that she finds it. Once she does, it is right there in the calm. It is the calm.

She has adapted her behavior to avoid the buzzing, the robotic voice. It's the learned response, a combination of a conscious and subconscious choice. She can't remember the moment she made the decision to suppress her emotions, but she has been consciously doing so for at least a few days, by her estimation. She tells herself it's nothing to be ashamed of, but she only has to say it because she feels shame. Sometimes such conditioning can be as detrimental as what it is meant to circumvent. Sometimes it can breed complacency.

Her anger flares, and she focuses on letting it burn instead of dousing it. But she is flinching even before the buzzing kicks in, anticipating the discomfort before it comes.

It takes it a moment—that lag again; she's noticed it half a dozen times since the first instance. She is certain it is not a fluke; it's a weakness. Even now, when she is not experiencing a mess of emotions, the device hesitates because there is both fear and anger, and it has to decide which to address first. In that moment she can clench her fist. It only lasts a second, maybe even a fraction of a second. But it might as well be forever for her. The programming catches up before she can act further. Her fingers uncurl.

"Oh," he says, just as the robotic voice begins its usual reminders about fear and anger. It is almost a chuckle. "Maybe I spoke too soon." He reaches over and turns on the radio, but she can't hear it over the chaos he has wrought in her brain.

One part of her will do anything to stop the buzzing, to never hear it again. Another part keeps fueling the anger to keep the sound going so she can't ignore it or her situation. But each buzz, each chastisement from the robotic voice, destroys parts of her. She can feel pieces crumbling; at some point it will be easier to adjust than to fight. She will have to get herself free before she forgets freedom altogether.

She has collected herself by the time the car pulls into his driveway, so the noise has faded to a dull hum in the background of her thoughts. She reminds herself to stay aware. But she can't afford to fight all the time and risk the slow burn to exhaustion. She needs to hold on to her emotions, protect them from his steady erosion and save them for the escape plan she is already formulating.

"Your new domain," he says as he leads her inside, and all her calm preparation is forgotten in an instant as she almost goes blind with fury.

`Rage is ugly`, the voice says as it cuts the legs out from under the feeling. It takes her a moment to come back to herself and another to pinpoint why his simple phrase enraged her more than almost anything else: it struck a dormant fault line deep within her, and in the process robbed her of a valuable asset for her plan.

She searches for the epicenter of the disruption while he leads her around the house and tells her—or rather, the device—what he expects of her while he is working on his career. Her internal hunt is a welcome distraction from her worsening external predicament, and it doesn't take her long to find the source. But it isn't as comforting or helpful as she had hoped.

His phrase angered her because she has heard similar sentiments from other people in her life, and in those instances she had believed them.

She chokes down tears and struggles for breath as the memories burst from her subconscious—all attracted to her current situation like iron shavings to a magnet. She snatches away the attached emotions before they can be detected, stuffs them into the small corner of her mind she has managed to block off for herself. For most of her adult life she has considered herself aware of the stereotypes, the societal pressure, the gender bias. She thought she had effectively fought against it, at least in her personal life. But for the first time she has seen it all stacked together, the direct comments from co-workers, the assumptions from friends and boyfriends couched in seemingly harmless statements, even the fact that no one intervened to ensure she had actually volunteered for this procedure. It is all woven through with a more pervasive message she hadn't consciously noticed. Combined, it has fueled a slower, more secretive erosion of her deeper sense of self.

But as the barrage abates, it clears much of the residue of these events away and reveals something useful. A gem hidden beneath the muck. Her tenuous plan for freedom comes into focus.

She is smarter than him, she has realized—no, remembered. She tries to trace the line back through her existence to find the moment she lost sight of herself, the turning point where what others told her about herself usurped her own knowledge. She is surprised when she can't pin it down—because it wasn't a single moment. It happened over time, from everyday exposure. Like paint fading over years in sunlight, her false self-image is another learned response caused by everyday exposure that went unnoticed because it happened in increments.

It has all contributed to her current situation. The overt and subtle messages that convinced a part of her of her inferiority also convinced the man of his superiority, led him to believe in the necessity of his invention.

She does not forgive him, does not feel sorry for him or excuse his behavior. But she has a clearer understanding of everything, and that understanding can only help.

That night, he rapes her again—he doesn't even pretend to get her consent by demanding a forced "yes" from her. Instead of trying to lock herself away in the safe corner of her mind, she stores all the pain and rage and disgust with the rest of her emotions.

"Remember," he says the next morning. "Don't leave the house." He has given her other commands: don't answer the door or the phone. Do the laundry, tidy up. Have dinner ready at 6:30. Secure that his instructions will be followed, he leaves for the lab. While her body goes about completing her assigned chores, her mind is planning her rescue.

That is how she finds another weakness in the device. Because she has begun storing her emotions, she has been separating them from their related thoughts. And she has found that the programming ignores thoughts that have no emotion behind them. So if she thinks *he is an asshole* in the way she might think *the sun is shining*—as a fact, not a heated opinion—it is read as logic, and thus as acceptable. The discovery allows her a certain amount of freedom in her cage.

She will only get one shot at escape. And maybe it's hubris, but she wants him to be there to see her succeed.

She suffers through four more days of his groping and commanding before she is confident enough in her plan to act. A part of her wonders if she could have implemented it sooner; she had all the steps figured out after two days. A bitter taste rises in her throat as she tries to decide which programming made her wait and endure more humiliation. But she stops herself from directing the frustration inward; he has put her in an extraordinary situation, and she has already extricated herself from her comfort zone in other ways.

Still, she can see the throughline in her life more clearly now that she has seen the deeper machinations at play within and without her, and this hesitation is not an isolated occurrence. She has spent significant portions of her life going well past the line of certainty before taking action. Sometimes it has been intentional, a preemptive move against anticipated criticism. She can no longer ignore the obvious, however: most of the time her reluctance to act on her own behalf was not a conscious strategic decision.

That subconscious mistrust of her own instincts led her to maintain a friendship with the man who did this to her well past the point she wanted—around the time he had first told her his idea for the device. But by then she had long absorbed the idea that any discomfort or unease was her being too sensitive. So she never called him out or cut him off, all the avoid hurting his feelings. After everything he's done, she isn't even sure he has any.

She quashes that thought—she doesn't want to start thinking of him as something other than human, to give him more power than he actually has. But she does promise herself that if her escape from him succeeds, the next thing she will do is free herself from the larger programming. It will be a long-term project, digging a tunnel through the mire over years instead of blowing it apart all at once. No matter how long it takes, she'll persevere until she can stand with all her real strengths and flaws—not the ones she's been convinced are hers by others. Until she is, unquestionably, her actual self.

She refocuses on her current task. She spends the day compartmentalizing, separating her actions from her emotions. Her stomach twists as she cannibalizes herself for the sake of her freedom; she feels more like a robot than she has at any other moment—and a part of her worries the process will be irreversible. But it is the linchpin of her plan, too necessary to avoid.

After she sanitizes her thoughts of emotions, she repeats the steps of the plan to herself. Over and over and over until they are a process, a fact, and thus accepted by the device. She will make dinner. They will eat.

Then he will want to have sex (*don't think rape, don't think rape* she repeats to herself, even if it is the correct word. She hasn't been able to strip the emotion from it). She will say no. Then she will talk to him about his prototype.

But as she is cleaning the dishes after dinner, with the first two steps of her plan flawlessly executed, her nerves set in. His lust radiates from him with an intensity to rival the summer sun, and the energy she needs to fend off her disgust leaves room for fear to worm in. If this doesn't work, she'll be stuck. He'll tweak his invention to eliminate her one loophole. Or maybe he put the lag in the program on purpose to set her up for this moment. Maybe she should wait a little longer, test it a little more. Her ambition and pride made her reckless; she shouldn't be trying to escape while he's home.

The buzzing fills her head. She closes her eyes to let the moment pass.

`Fear is unwarranted`, the voice tells her—the first time it has said something useful. It has overridden society's brainwashing, which speaks in her own voice and spikes her blood with doubt.

Then his hands are on her hips, his mouth on her neck, and she can't wait another moment.

"Take off your clothes," he says. It's meant to be coy, but a threat lurks in his tone. Her hands twitch to obey. She stops them with one word; the word she has been longing to speak:

"No."

He tenses against her. One, two, three hot breaths against her neck. She stifles the urge to rush through the remaining steps now that freedom is so close. The next part of the plan will be the most difficult.

He grabs her shoulder and spins her around to face him, his eyes wide. "What?"

"No." The word feels good on her tongue, even with the awful electronic quality in her voice.

"How are you doing this?" he demands, his face red. Spittle flies from his lips and lands on her face. She almost loses it then. For a moment the buzzing crescendos as her revulsion seeps out of its compartment, and she's certain she's ruined her plan. If the programming disables her now, even momentarily, he'll make sure she doesn't get another chance.

She takes a slow breath. *Talk to him about his prototype,* she reminds herself. Her loathing tucks itself away again. As the buzzing fades, she reaches up a hand and wipes the spit from her face.

"I'm smarter than you," she says, as much for her sake as for his. With that final fact spoken, she rips opens the Pandora's box of her emotions. She doesn't steel herself, doesn't give the man or his contraption any hint of what is about to come.

The fury, the fear, the desolation, the disgust all weave together and rush through her, a stampede crushing everything else. After almost two weeks of emotional suppression and dissection, the elation of experiencing all her feelings at once is euphoric.

He is so shocked he is frozen, sputtering. She manages a satisfied smirk as the buzzing in her head reaches its apex. Then it is drowning out her thoughts, trying to combat her emotional assault. But it's overwhelmed, as she'd hoped. Only he would make a device just like himself: so rudimentary it couldn't handle the reality of a human being.

A warmth begins to spread from the base of her neck up her skull. At first it's almost pleasant, like the effect of a couple of cocktails. But it keeps getting hotter, becoming uncomfortable, then unbearable. Lava injected into her brain.

She screams and braces herself against the table. A look of concern and fright passes over his face. Then her vision goes white as her insides burn.

She might not survive, but she is willing to die trying to reclaim herself.

Her ears ring from the force of her own screaming, and the acrid stench of singed hair sears her nostrils. That's when the numbness sets in, dousing her agony along the same path it started. Either she is approaching death or she has survived, but it is another few moments before it's clear which way her fate has tipped.

The world filters back in through the white. She is alive.

Her throat is raw; each shaking breath she pulls in stings, but still her lungs struggle for enough oxygen for her overstrained body. She is shivering so badly she can feel it in her bones. But she is free.

He has recoiled from her, as if she has morphed into some unknown beast. She has succeeded, but she isn't sure what to do next. The self-confidence that conquered his prototype is crumbling in her desperate grasp; her mind is a smoldering landscape that needs time to blossom again. Time she doesn't have.

"Natalie?" he asks, moving a few steps closer to her than she would like. There is real concern on his face, a softness around his eyes. But then some thought strikes him—she can't pretend to know what it might be—and the gentleness disappears as his expression shifts to something more sinister.

But she is still hung up on him saying her name. It knocks her out of her stupor, the sheer revulsion of that one word coming from his mouth. She embraces the feeling, even if there is a small part of her cowering, waiting for the buzzing and the robotic voice.

He reaches for her with a closed fist, not to comfort but to cause harm. She steps back, almost stumbling, until she is out of his reach. Then she takes a wide stance and steps forward, throwing a punch of her own. Her fist catches him on the side of his face, close enough to the trigeminal nerve—pure luck. But she thinks she's earned that much. He stumbles back, then drops to the floor, unconscious. Just like that, she's in control of him. His fate is in her hands.

"Don't ever say my name again, asshole," she spits. She lets the words ring in her ears for a moment—savoring the absence of the electronic quality. She had almost forgotten the sound of her own voice.

Then she steps over him and heads for the door. A part of her wants to stay and throttle the life out of him, but that would make her too similar to him. Now that she has seen herself more clearly and thoroughly than she has in a long while, she doesn't want to lose herself again.

Besides, she has everything she needs for a more satisfying justice. Her continued existence will be his undoing.

Countdown

Kaitlyn Sudol

J esus, Kath, where the hell are you taking me?"

Lynn does *not* stutter or pant through the question, which is a little victory she has no shame clinging to. They've been walking for fifteen minutes, the last five of them on an overgrown off-shoot of the main path. Most of the walking has been uphill. Lynn is wearing flip-flops. Katherine is an asshole.

"Almost, almost," Kath says, and squeezes her fingers. It's enough to placate Lynn, as much as she hates to admit it. Every little touch, every little gesture has silenced her almost immediately over the past two weeks. It's like there's a clock in her brain counting down and the ticking gets louder every time Katherine reminds her how much she loves her.

It's only another minute of walking before the path opens, maybe another minute after that until the trees fall away. They're on the top of a hill in a clearing. Katherine drops her hand, and Lynn turns in a slow circle, taking it all in.

"Okay, Dr. Wong, you win. This is beautiful," she admits, grudgingly.

"I know." Katherine is so fucking full of herself sometimes.

When Lynn looks back, Katherine has pulled a blanket out of her backpack and spread it on the ground. Her lunchbox is holding down one end, the stupid squishy bag that's shaped vaguely like Chewbacca's chest. It's furry. Lynn hates it. Kath has had it as long as Lynn has known her and takes it everywhere.

And there's that ticking again.

"Baby, sit down," Kath says, dropping gracefully to the blanket and sitting cross-legged with one swift movement. Lynn groans.

"Sitting on the ground is garbage, Kath," she says, but she does it, because Kath could ask her to do anything right now and she would do it in a heartbeat.

171

Well, almost anything.

Katherine busies herself pulling things out of her lunchbox—apple slices, sandwiches, string cheese. Out of her backpack comes a bottle of moderately expensive champagne and two plastic glasses. An elementary school lunch with quality booze—that's her Katherine.

"This is your big date idea?" Lynn says, accepting a sandwich. "A picnic in the dark in the woods. I'd think you'd want to avoid being serial killed for the next two weeks."

"You watch too many shitty horror movies," Kath says. "Tell me about school today."

Lynn picks at her sandwich—turkey, honey mustard, cheese, and tomatoes. Her favorite.

"School was school," she says. "I've learned about half the kids' names. Angie doesn't like the new guy on our team. I taught my littlest guy how to tie his shoes and he untied them three times over the course of the day so he could re-tie them and run up to show me." It's useless to fight her smile at that. Amal, his name is, and he's a peanut and she's not supposed to pick favorites, but she doesn't think there's a teacher in the history of the world who's come out of a school year without at least one secret favorite in their heart.

"Angie doesn't like guys in general," Kath says. "I can't believe she manages to stay married to one."

"Seriously," Lynn says. "He's harmless, just, you know, young and full of ideas. Bureaucracy hasn't ground him down yet."

"Bureaucracy hasn't ground you down yet," Kath says, and Lynn rolls her eyes. "Don't do that. You know it's true. You're adorably idealistic."

"I'm realistic and I have ideals," Lynn says. "Those are two different things."

Kath hums, smiling her stupid, butter-wouldn't-melt smile. There are times Lynn wants to throttle her. Strangely, they frequently intersect with the times Lynn loves her the most.

"I like your face," she says, and leans over to press a kiss to Kath's cheek, just because she can.

"I like yours too, sweets," Kath says.

Lynn talks a little more about school as they finish their sandwiches. Kath talks about the mountains and mountains of paperwork she spent the day filling out. They argue about some stupid movie they saw over the weekend and speculate about Lynn's brother's vague Facebook posts. Kath leans against Lynn's side, tucking herself under her arm the way she always has. Lynn runs her hands through Kath's long, soft, dark hair and tries to drown out the ticking and just enjoy the moment.

The champagne has only just been poured when Katherine gives in and gets poetic.

"This is why I brought you up here, you know," she says. She's gesturing to the sky above them. Lynn has to admit that it's a beautiful view; there are at least twice as many stars as they can see from home.

"It's pretty nice," Lynn says with a sigh.

"Baby, you can't blame the stars for this. You know that."

Lynn tilts her head back and stares up at the sky, blinking hard to keep herself from tearing up like an idiot.

"Shut up," she says quietly.

Katherine sits up, taps her fingernail against the plastic cup of champagne.

"Here's the thing about the big bang," she says. Lynn groans. She can groan with her mouth closed. If she opens it, she's either going to laugh or sob and she's not sure which, so groaning is the safest bet. At least Kath's voice drowns out the ticking. "So, there's a lot of physics mumbo jumbo that I know you and your art degree don't care about, but essentially, we can trace back to the Big Bang by essentially backtracking relativity to a finite point in the past where the rules of physics just fall apart. The singularity, right?"

"Art degree, remember?" Lynn manages to say without her voice breaking.

"Right, right, I love your art degree," Kath says. "So, the point is, there's a point where everything wasn't and then we have the singularity and the universe expanding—going from basically nothing to something, right? Huge, crazy temperatures and crazy pressure and the basically nothing that we start with goes out and out and out and forms subatomic particles, forms atoms, forms. . . everything. Eventually. Particle and antiparticles created and destroyed, matter and antimatter. . . lots of things and their opposites, basically, chaos and it was *beautiful*. We think it was beautiful. The math is beautiful."

"Physicists are weird," Lynn says.

"You would think it's beautiful too," Kath promises. "When I get back—well, we'll figure out a way to show you how beautiful it is. It's just another art form, baby. But that's not the point. The point is that we have basically nothing and from that basically nothing, we get everything else. Every single thing originates there, every single piece of matter. That matter in the trees around us, the matter in this champagne. Right?"

"Katherine, this really isn't the time for a physics lesson," Lynn says. She takes a long, shuddering breath. "Can we talk about anything else, please?"

"I have a point," Kath says. She leans over and presses a long kiss to Lynn's temple. "I promise."

Lynn sighs and squeezes her eyes shut. That's Katherine's way, that's her fucking way. She can talk herself into anything, can make everyone listen to her until she's said her piece. She always has to explain herself. She never fucking stops talking. Lynn used to think that was cute.

"So, matter, right? That's where we left off," Kath continues. "All matter is created—and I'm skipping a few billion years, here—but the long and short of this is that the same basically nothing that started the Big Bang, the same everything that's come from it—it's always been the same. And it started the same place. So the things that make up the stars, every single one of them? They're the same things that make up you and me."

Lynn opens her eyes again. Kath is staring at her with a soft, gentle expression. Lynn can't look at her—she looks up at the sky again, at the stupid stars.

"So when I'm up there," Kath continues, "I'm going to be up there surrounded by the same stuff that we're made up of. I'm going to be up there surrounded by the stars, which are made up of the same things that make up you and me. I'm going to be all the way up there, but I'll still be surrounded by pieces of you, by pieces of your component parts. And you'll be surrounded by pieces of me. We won't be apart, not really."

"That's so dumb, Kath," Lynn says. She covers her face with her hands and tries to keep her breathing even. "That's beautiful and poetic and whatever the fuck, but that doesn't make you any less gone. That doesn't make our apartment any less empty, it doesn't make our *bed* any less empty." *It doesn't make my heart any less empty*, she wants to say.

She doesn't. She promised Kath she was done being dramatic after last weekend's fiasco.

Kath's arms wrap around her, holding her close. She rests her head on Kath's chest and hugs her back and wills herself not to cry. They have two weeks left. Two whole weeks. She needs to throw herself into them instead of spending them mourning. She'll have five whole years to mourn once Kath is gone.

"Oh, baby," Kath says. She rocks Lynn back and forth. "Oh, sweetheart. I have to go. I have to go, baby."

Lynn takes a deep breath and pulls away and swallows back a scream because she can't do this now. She's already yelled. She's already thrown a tantrum. She's already sobbed. She has to spend these next two weeks *present* before time runs out.

"I know that, Katherine," she snaps, rubbing fiercely at her eyes and sitting up again. "I fucking know."

They sit in silence for a few moments. Lynn finishes her champagne and lets the empty plastic cup roll off the edge of the blanket. She pulls her knees up against her chest. Katherine stretches her legs out and leans back on her elbows, staring up at the sky.

"I love you so much, Lynnae," Katherine says.

"I know," Lynn says. She sighs. "I love you too. That's why I want you to go. Even though it really *fucking* sucks."

Katherine sits up again. Her hand rests innocuously on the blanket between them, but Lynn has known her long enough to recognize how deliberate the movement is. She counts to ten in her head, right along with the ticking, and then reaches out and puts her hand on top of Kath's.

Around them, crickets chirp. Something rustles deep in the woods. Something flutters in the branches of the trees. The night is cool and quiet and calm and Kath's hand is small and warm under her own. Lynn breathes in and out and even lets herself look up and appreciate the stars.

"Do you remember the night we met?" Kath asks, apropos of nothing.

"I remember you used the stupidest line of all time."

"It was not stupid!"

"'I'm an astronaut, you know.'"

"I was stating a fact! I'd just started in the program! I was excited! I wasn't trying to use it for. . . for sex!"

"It worked though."

Kath laughs, high and light. "It did," she agrees. "I couldn't believe it. After you fell asleep I sat up in bed and tried to figure out how I tricked you into taking me home. You were so beautiful—I was shocked."

"I was a chubby green-haired grad student," Lynn says. She's glad it's dark enough to hide her blush, even though she should have long since gotten over the pleased embarrassment at hearing Kath call her beautiful. "Now I'm a chubby brown-haired teacher. You didn't exactly win the lottery. I, on the other hand, bagged me an astronaut."

Kath laughs again, as Lynn intended.

"You had so many freckles," Kath says dreamily. She leans over until their shoulders bump together. "I love them so much. Like galaxies across your skin. Like stars."

"You're so weird," Lynn says. She bumps their shoulders together again.

"I look up at the stars and I think of you, you know? Which seems silly. I was studying the stars for so long before I met you. But you changed it. I have no idea how—it doesn't make any logical sense. It's true, though; I look at the stars and I think of you."

Lynn doesn't know what to say to that. She doesn't know that there's anything to say.

"I'm going to be up there," Kath continues, "surrounded by stars. Thinking of you. Which doesn't seem fair. You should have something to think of me."

Lynn can feel Kath shifting her weight. She glances over in time to see Kath pull a red velvet box out of her pocket. She snaps it open one handed and pulls out the ring inside. Lynn feels a thousand arguments bubble up inside of her. All that comes out is a small, aggravated noise.

Kath holds the ring out to her.

"Katherine, we had this conversation last week," Lynn says. She stares at the ring and doesn't take it. It's so unassuming. In her memories of last weekend, it feels. . . bigger. More imposing.

"I know," Kath says.

"I'm not gonna spend five years engaged and alone."

"I know."

"I'm not gonna accept a proposal because you think it's the right thing to do before you leave for half a decade."

"I know. And I'm not proposing again."

"Good," Lynn says. Somewhere on the other side of the country, her mother is weeping and doesn't know why.

"I'm saying take it," Kath says. "Hold onto it while I'm gone. Give it back to me in five years."

Lynn looks from Kath to the ring to Kath to the ring. Kath raises her eyebrows expectantly.

The root issue isn't the ring. It was never the ring. It's not that Lynn doesn't love Kath, either, because Lynn would kill for Katherine if she asked. It's the expectation of the thing. It's the resignation. *Welp, I'm going off to space for five to six years, so I'll ask you to marry me so you don't feel like I'm dumping you for my career.* She knows, mostly, that's not what Kath was thinking, but the feeling persists. The pity she can imagine feeling when people see the ring and know that Katherine's not coming home for a long time.

At least military spouses get to stay on the same planet when their husbands and wives are doing their ultra-dangerous jobs. Fucking outer space. Jesus. The reality of dating an astronaut is scarier than she ever could have imagined that night at the bar all those years ago.

It's not the ring and it's not that she doesn't love Katherine. It's not that she doesn't want to marry Katherine. It's everything else—the baggage, the distance, the ache in her chest that isn't going to be filled up by a piece of jewelry. It's the performance of it. It's the inevitability. It's the title she'll have to live with for five years on her own.

But holding onto the promise is different than wearing it on her finger. Keeping it safe and alive—well, Lynn was going to do that anyway. Lynn is already planning to spend the next five years keeping the spark in her chest warm and protected and waiting for Kath to come home and nurture it back to life. She may be made of stardust, but Katherine is the one who knows the secret to making her heart shine strong and bright. That's not going to change, not if she's gone for five years or fifteen.

She takes the ring. Sighs. Shoves it in her pocket.

"I'm going to plan a really embarrassing public proposal," she warns Katherine. "You'll be mortified."

"I could never be mortified about marrying you, my Lynnae," Katherine says with the sort of sincerity only she can muster.

"You say that now, but I'm gonna have five years to perfect it," Lynn says.

Kath crawls closer and puts her arms around Lynn, hugging her close. "I can't wait."

Lynn sighs again and goes back to running her fingers through Kath's hair, letting Kath shove her around until she's lying back on the blanket with Kath lying half on top of her. Typical Kath. She always gets what she wants one way or another.

It's lucky that what she wants so often aligns with what Lynn wants, too.

The ticking is quiet for the first time in weeks, a soft background noise instead of the constant thrum of her anxiety. It's not, she thinks, ticking down two weeks to something ending anymore—it's ticking down five years to something beginning.

Lynn can't wait either.